The Freethinker's Daughter

Also by Jenny O'Neill (as Jenny Davis)

Goodbye and Keep Cold
Sex Education
Checking on the Moon

The Freethinker's Daughter

A Novel by

Jenny O'Neill

OLD COVE PRESS

LEXINGTON, KENTUCKY

Published by
Old Cove Press • oldcove.com

Distributed by
Ohio University Press • ohioswallow.com

Paperback ISBN: 978-1-956855-00-5
Electronic ISBN: 978-1-956855-01-2

First Edition

The Freethinker's Daughter was designed by Nyoka Hawkins.
The type is Century Oldstyle, designed by Morris Fuller Benton
in 1909, and Adobe Caslon, designed by Carol Twombly in 1990.
Cover painting by Pam Oldfield Meade, 2021.
Grateful acknowledgment to Stephanie Adams and Sharon Hatfield.

Library of Congress Cataloging-in-Publication Data
Names: O'Neill, Jenny, author.
Title: The Freethinker's daughter : a novel / Jenny O'Neill.
Description: Lexington, Kentucky : Old Cove Press, 2022. |
Audience: Ages 12+. | Audience: Grades 7–9. | Summary: When
a flash flood destroys her family's Lexington, Kentucky, home,
thirteen-year-old Cal Farmer goes into domestic service in a
wealthy family's mansion, where she witnesses firsthand the
brutalities of slavery.
Identifiers: LCCN 2021049883 (print) | LCCN 2021049884 (ebook) |
ISBN 9781956855005 (paperback) | ISBN 9781956855012 (pdf)
Subjects: CYAC: Coming of age—Fiction. | Orphans—Fiction.
| Free thought—Fiction. | Household employees—Fiction. |
Slavery—Fiction. | Lexington (Ky.)—Fiction. | Kentucky—
History—1792–1865—Fiction. | LCGFT: Novels. | Historical fiction.
Classification: LCC PZ7.O55314 Fr 2022 (print) | LCC PZ7.O55314
(ebook) | DDC [Fic]—dc23
LC record available at https://lccn.loc.gov/2021049883
LC ebook record available at https://lccn.loc.gov/2021049884

For Marjorie Guyon, whose breathtaking paintings awakened Cal and spurred me to tell her story. And to the thousands and thousands of Africans who were sold in front of Lexington's courthouse.

And as everything is, for CDO.

Contents

Chapter I
The Flood • 3

Chapter II
Away from Home • 15

Chapter III
Mama • 25

Chapter IV
Tweeny • 35

Chapter V
My First Visit Home • 47

Chapter VI
Something Daring • 55

Chapter VII
A Spring Surprise • 65

Chapter VIII
Cholera • 73

Chapter IX

Rosalie • 83

Chapter X

Rose • 89

Chapter XI

Sad and Mad • 95

Chapter XII

A Choice • 107

Chapter XIII

Charity Begins at Home • 119

Chapter XIV

Lawton • 131

Chapter XV

Melancholia • 141

Chapter XVI

The Orphan Asylum • 147

Chapter XVII

Aunt Charlotte's Gift • 159

Chapter XVIII

A Trip to the Theater • 169

Chapter XIX

Asylum • 177

Chapter XX

Changes • 187

Chapter XXI

A Happy Surprise • 195

Chapter XXII

The History of My Life So Far • 207

The Freethinker's Daughter

Chapter I

The Flood

The night of the flood, Mr. Davis met his maker. His was the only fatality, although I'd put my childhood up as the next-in-line contender. My life as a child with Mama and my brother Jackie on Second Creek washed out with all the other debris.

Miss Em, our goat, floated away and we never did see her again, so maybe she died too, but most likely she found footing in some other county. We lost a few chickens but most of them managed to ride the wave out. But for me, the flood changed everything. I was taken completely by surprise, and I've noticed since then that life tends to career and crash along at its own pace, in any direction at all, satisfying whatever whims it wants and entirely without my consent.

It started like this: Mama and Jackie and I were lying in Mama's big bed. They were sleeping. I was listening to the *plunk plunk* of water dripping into the buckets we set carefully around the house. On the roof and all around us, rain pounded down. The creek had been rising for days but there was no particular reason for concern. Pa had built our place up above the high water mark of the 1819 flood, and all my life we'd never had any trouble. Our house was just two rooms and a porch, but for me it had always been home.

I listened to Jackie, breathing softly, humming a little in his sleep. I loved how he did that, as though sleep for him was full of music. I nuzzled his head to smell his milky curls. Mama was curled on her side, her arm protectively around us. I, sleepless as I so often am, lay listening and letting my mind become fuzzy and soft. I was drowsing and kind of letting the raindrops sing me to sleep, when I heard Mr. Combs from up the creek hollering to "Get *up!*" and "Get *out!*" His voice sounded panicked.

"Run! Run!" he was yelling as he passed us by, and quick as a spark Mama jerked up and grabbed hold of me by the scruff of the neck. "Hurry!" she hissed as she pillowed Jackie into her body and swept all three of us out the door and up the hill as fast as we could go. I couldn't see anything but nightclothes and mud as we pulled at the hill and climbed barefooted and panting. There were weeds and stone clumps I grasped at and even though I kept sliding back I slowly made progress. My feet were freezing and torn in places from the rocks but I could barely feel them.

Once, I did glance behind and saw a wall of water coming down the creek. Literally. It was crashing in on us, tumbling toward us. I screamed. Aunt Charlotte came out of her house and we all started a mad climb up the cliff face. It isn't sheer but it's steep and we clawed at handholds and trees and clumps of weeds to pull ourselves up and up, away from the rushing water below. Mama held Jackie and climbed too, we were spitting mud, gasping for breath and handhold, foothold, desperate to keep going: up, up, faster. I heard nothing but the sobbing of my own breath as it tore in and out of my chest. The rain lashed us and the thistles, bushes, thorns, and twigs tore at our clothes and skin. I felt none of the scratches and tears, felt no injury, felt nothing but stark panic and furious determination to get to the top.

I do not know how long we climbed. I only remember tumbling onto the street at the top of the hill. Mama and Jackie, who was crying, were lying there already, and Aunt Charlotte called for me to help her up the last few feet. I pulled on her hand and she finally came to safety. Mr. and Mrs. Norman were up there too, but I don't know where. We lay utterly limp on the streaming cobblestones of High Street gasping for air, willing our hearts to slow and our senses to return to us. The rain pounded and I was almost unconscious for a few minutes. A profound exhaustion was claiming me, but first Mama and Jackie and then Aunt Charlotte came to me and sat me up and hugged me and warmed me—or tried to—with their own soaking freezing bodies. None of us had breath to speak and Jackie cried until he cried out and we huddled there, shuddering in shock and shivering with cold, still trying to take in what had just happened.

I really don't know how much time passed before other people came, holding lanterns and shouting. Between the raindrops I saw figures in the night standing above us. Someone opened up the church and we were ushered in, where we sat huddled in the dark pews. It was cold, being late March, and for a long while, Mama just kept rubbing my legs and patting Jackie on his hands. He played a little with her fingers. In the middle of all that misery, Jackie was just a baby and wanted to make fun. It took a long time of just panting and shivering and catching our breath before we could do anything else. I was only wearing my nightgown so when there came a lady down the church aisle with a blanket, Mama quickly saw to it that I held on to Jackie and we were both wrapped up and warmed.

I saw Missy, who I knew slightly from early childhood when our mothers did wash together, walking behind a beautiful lady, the most beautiful I had ever seen up until then. The lady was tall and golden, jewels sparkled in her ears and she was richly clothed. She smelled of powder and perfume and her cloak swirled around her, defining her space. She stood above us and urged us to take the clothes they had brought. We made tents out of our arms to shield each other and changed into strangers' clothes.

"You must," Aunt Charlotte scolded me when I modestly resisted. "Otherwise, honey, you could catch your death of cold." Death had a new sharp and uncomfortable meaning for me now and I quickly patted myself dry and put on the mismatched clothes people

6

had brought. I have never been as cold as I was that night. I piled on clothes, wore two or three layers of dresses and still couldn't get warm.

Mama left me petting on Jackie and moved out into the aisle. People all around us were groaning and murmuring quietly. I heard crying and even some soft singing. Jackie, who had been screaming in terror as we ran, was now sitting up and looking eagerly at the people in the pews. He was an easy baby, always interested in whatever was happening around him, and I was just glad to have him in my arms.

There were people in the church from all up and down Second Creek, which is a little leg off Town Branch that runs through Lexington. Later, we learned there was a break in a dam in Maysville, which is up river from us. The water built up so fast it was huge before anyone knew it. Flash flood they call it. The wall I saw was real. It was over twenty feet high and slamming into us. I never knew until then that water could rise up like a monster and devour you, but it can.

No one knew what remained of our lives below. Could our small house have withstood such a battering? There was no way yet to know. "We have to hold ourselves in patience," Mama counseled when I voiced my thoughts.

The ladies of the Hill organized tea and cakes and broth, which were taken around to us by slaves holding huge silver platters with cups and saucers and bowls and spoons. The smell and warmth of the soup made me feel like crying. The lantern light in the church flickered, the fire in the stove began to roar, and as the building warmed and people recovered, some children began to run up and down the aisles, laughing. There slowly developed an almost festive mood as people told their stories of what had happened over and over, newly aware of our fortunate escape. We all looked somewhat comical dressed in other people's clothing and sometimes we would start smiling over nothing. In spite of—or maybe because of—our narrow escape, our spirits rose and at times we were giddy. At some time during the night, we realized Mr. Davis wasn't among us and a long somber moment followed as we contemplated the old man's fate.

The men gathered in the back of the church where they passed a flask of something stronger than tea and coughed and stamped numb feet and talked in deep voices. Mama had made Jackie a little pallet on the pew and he was sleeping at last.

The golden woman from the Hill, which is what we on Second Creek called High Street, came to us with fresh tea. Behind her was Missy, who I now understood was this lady's slave. I had never thought of her as a slave back when we played and told secrets and raced each other down the bank of the creek. I met her eye and could see she remembered me too, but beyond a slight flicker of the eyes, she made no sign.

The lady who had so bedazzled me was called Mrs. Hunt-Adams. She was the most beautiful, elegant, and sweet-smelling woman I had ever seen in my life. Her thick honey-colored hair shimmered in the

8

candlelight, her eyes were warm and smiling as she bent over to talk to us. Mama and Aunt Charlotte thanked her for the provisions as Missy poured tea and passed our cups.

"And who is this?" she asked, addressing me. Her voice was like her hair, multicolored shades of gold.

I could feel myself blushing. "Calendula Farmer, ma'am," I answered.

"Calendula?" she asked. "Like the flower?"

"Yes, ma'am," I managed, and that was the full extent of our conversation, but when she turned back to Mama, Mrs. Hunt-Adams murmured something I couldn't quite hear. Mama stood up and the two of them walked to an empty pew further down.

Aunt Charlotte and I sat there, Jackie sleeping between us. Finally warm and full, I almost didn't care what they were talking about. I watched their two heads incline toward each other. How different they were. Mama's brown hair, which was just beginning to fleck with gray, was dry now but still straggly from the rain and the mud of our climb. It contrasted with Mrs. Hunt-Adams's pale blonde perfection.

I did not know it but while I was catching my breath, Mama was arranging my life. Maybe it was ten minutes and maybe it was fifteen, but Mama came back around to the pew where we were and said, "Calendula, you have a job."

I was stunned. A job? Me?

Mama was saying something and I pulled my attention back to her. "You'll be the wage earner in the

9

family, Cal, not the way it's supposed to be, you being just thirteen, but still. Needs must." She looked away from me then and I knew she was thinking of Pa, who for too long now had been not only absent but unheard from completely. Just then the silence of his absence roared. "You'll bring home a dollar a week, Cal, and it's money we badly need. With this flood," she gestured to the roof where we could still hear the rain pounding, "it's untelling what is left back home." She stopped and took a breath and then, speaking low but with force, she said, "I don't see another way." She sighed. "And perhaps it's Providence, in fact it probably is, our need being so great and her offer coming just now. At any rate, you will go with her tonight."

"No!" I blurted before I could control myself. "I mean, Mama, what about you and Jackie? Our house. There are just so many things." Without thinking, I said, "Mama, you need me right now." I turned to Aunt Charlotte for support and it was when I saw her sad face that I knew she agreed with Mama. Needs must.

"Daughter," Mama said in a low voice. She reached to take my hand and I had to stop myself from flinching away. But of anger and hurt—both of which I felt—it was hurt she was soothing by holding my hand, and I surprised myself by clutching at her with a desperation I would have thought myself too old for. "Cal," she said. She waited, and I knew she was waiting for me to meet her eyes, and I finally did but it was hard. "What I need from you right now is to take up this burden, shoulder it with dignity, and continue on with your life."

My face must have betrayed some of my shock and surprise. Continue on with my life? My life as I knew it was over.

"You are to get a half day free every week." She laughed a thin chuckle. "It was supposed to be a half day every two weeks but as a kindness to me"—her eyebrows rose in a gesture of irony, as though she deserved no kindness, no special consideration—"she decided to let you have a half day every week and an hour a week for your studies. So that's all to the good, isn't it?"

This last was said in a way that made me realize she wasn't at all insensitive to my feelings but help-less to change what faced us. Jackie woke and began to fuss. Mama nursed him briefly, then handed him to me. "Tell him you'll be back," she instructed and I saw her eyes glisten with unshed tears. Feeling her pain, as I had been able to do all my life, stabbed me with remorse at my own selfishness. Before I could stop myself, I began to sob. Trying to stop, I got the hiccups but kept crying. Sometimes, tears come and there is no stopping them, try though I might. This was one of those times. Mama hugged us both as I soaked my brother's curls with hot salty tears. Jackie didn't cry but rather seemed to like being in a sand-wich composed of his mother and weeping sister.

There was nothing more to say so we stopped talking. Eventually, I saw Mrs. Hunt-Adams, with Missy in tow, sweeping up the aisle to where we sat in the pews. Still holding Jackie, I slid out as did

Mama before me and Aunt Charlotte behind. We all embraced, a tangle of arms and heads and hearts. My crying had ceased and I was as ready as I could be to meet what came next.

Aunt Charlotte mumbled into my neck, "You be a good girl, Cal, you hear me?" I nodded. Aunt Charlotte would be mortified to learn of any misbehavior or—heaven forbid—laziness on my part. "Make us proud, sweetness," she said. I felt new tears threaten and I pulled apart to gain control. It never occurred to me to do anything but follow my mother's dictums. Keep learning, do your best with dignity, and continue on with your life. From Aunt Charlotte, behave and work hard. Make us proud.

Turning to face my future as well as Mrs. Hunt-Adams, I was struck anew by the elegant beauty of her. She held herself effortlessly and perfectly erect. Even at this hour after many hours in the now-overheated church, she looked cool and clean. The fall of honey hair that was caught in a bun seemed as perfectly coiffed as when she came in. Even Missy looked better than I in her plain but clean shift and cloak. As I stood ready to go, I felt ridiculous and painfully self-conscious in layers of ill-fitting clothes and too tight shoes that belonged to someone else.

We were met at the church door by an elderly black man I came to know as Lawton. He put up an umbrella and ushered Mrs. Hunt-Adams, and to a lesser extent Missy and me, across the street and into the mansion that would become my home for the next many months.

I realize now Mama sent me out to work to save our family, not to get rid of me, but there was a place in my thirteen-year-old heart where I harbored an unseemly self-pity and a guilty, unfair anger at my mother that no amount of self-recrimination or reasoning seemed to ease.

Well, if it was to be so, so be it.

And this is how I became employed as a tweeny in Mrs. Hunt-Adams's household. Sudden, yes, but the flood had washed all the usual markers of time and custom away. Later, we found out our house on Second Creek still stood, but everything in it was gone.

Chapter II

Away from Home

That first night in the Hunt-Adams house was very lonely. It was dawn when I stumbled up the steep back stairway behind Cook—who was now my boss—up four flights of steps to a narrow alcove on the fourth floor. The room was clean but quite small, and although I like to think myself brave, I was scared. Two iron beds stood against the wall and two small chests stood in front of them. The ceiling tilted in and I could see I would have to crouch not to bump my head. In the place where the slanting eaves met there was a small oval window.

"Now you be quiet," Cook puffed, although I had said nothing and she was the one breathing heavily. "That is Mrs. Alice," she whispered, nodding at the slim sleeping form in front of us. "You'll meet her in the morning."

I knew no one and had no friends in this strange house. Lying scared and sad in a strange bed with a strange woman breathing quietly beside me, I let my mind drift back to just the other day when I had skipped

15

home from school carefree and happy as I've ever been. The cold had doubled down in January, and February was uncommonly cruel with ice and snow, then teasingly warm for a day or two. Those warm days, Mama sent me out to the garden patch to prepare to sow seeds and plant potatoes. Cold makes everything harder.

This was the world of my childhood, the world of my mother, a hard-working, free-thinking, proud citizen of the new nation, and of her adopted town, Lexington, Kentucky, a thriving, growing frontier city in 1833 with a prosperous tobacco and hemp business. The city had much to boast of, including the first university in the west (Transylvania), which had a famous and renowned medical school. Most beloved by the City Fathers was the title "Athens of the West" for so proud were we of our culture, music, art, literature, and theater. Less often bragged about is that we had the first institution for the insane in the West, but it is a first nonetheless.

1833 was a year of great changes. My world would tilt and nothing would ever go back to the way it had been. A chasm opened up and the landscape has never been the same. And this wasn't just my experience. All of Lexington reeled under the blows of that year.

As I lay in my new bed, willing sleep to find me, I thought back to my day of victory at school in January. To think how excited I was; I was actually skipping home from Dame School. I'd been chosen to receive— no, I had won—the Singing Prize, won it after multiple tests and competitions, won it that day. I had plucked my victory from the hands of Ambrosia Brooks, my closest challenger. Thus it was I who won the honor to sing the new song "My Country, 'Tis of Thee" to Andrew Jackson, President of the United States, when he would travel to Lexington for the Fourth of July festivities. My success was no small achievement.

The President's coming was an event much looked forward to and had already been talked about by everyone in town. Even in January, the President's visit was on our minds, and suddenly, miraculously, I was to be an actual part of history. I was so proud my buttons were practically busting, and I could hardly contain my excitement as I hurried home to tell Mama, the lines of the song's first verse singing in my head:

My country, 'tis of thee
Sweet land of liberty
Of thee I sing

I knew Mama would be tickled because she'd just had a letter from a cousin in Boston that the song had been sung at a Children's Festival up there. (People didn't seem to mind that the tune was the same as "God Save the King.")

King Solomon saw me as I turned onto the path that leads up to our house on Second Creek. How can I explain who William "King" Solomon is? His name itself is a jest, implying conversely he is a fool, but he isn't. He does get mixed up sometimes, but he also gets a lot of things right. As for drinking, the man is a natural wonder. He has always, or for so long it might as well have been always, been the town drunk, but that label doesn't do him justice. King is a little bit simple but not stupid by any means, and he is almost always somewhat drunk. He is a fixture in Lexington. He became a hero, but it changed him not at all. He wore his honor lightly and bashfully. He does odd jobs for just about everyone and gets paid in whiskey and cigars, his two main requirements for a happy life.

And King does seem to live a reasonably happy life. He is friends with everyone in town. He and Aunt Charlotte came here with the Clays and the Hunts when they traveled from Virginia back in 1815 or so, before I was born. Aunt Charlotte is a free black woman and King is white, but she was the one who had a house next door to ours and a business selling baked goods in the market, not to mention a horse and cart.

King was more or less homeless, although once the city built the new courthouse with a spanking fine jail, he'd been its number one citizen. He could always be picked up as publicly intoxicated because he always was. King didn't get drunk like some people do, not in a mean way. My own father was a drunk like that, drink inflamed him, but King just kept on being himself. I have known him my whole life and loved him always. He is a powerfully built, entirely gentle, rumpled old man, who smells of cigars and whiskey but whose smile is sweet and whose words are always soft. He is as strong as a bull and taller by far than most men, and as long as he has his whiskey to keep him going, he does work. He is liked by everyone except the jailer who resented him taking up jail space in the winter. King and I actually share the same birthday, January 1st. "You and me and the finest horseflesh in the country," he likes to say.

That day, he spied me and called out, "Look at my girl Calendula," as I skipped up the path toward home.

"King!" I shouted, happy that he should be the first to hear my incredible news. "King, I am going to sing for the President!" It came out as an explosion of words, and I became suddenly, if only momentarily, shy.

King was impressed. He rocked back in his broken-down boots, stared up at the sky a minute. His gray eyebrows raised and waggled, he opened his mouth to speak but didn't say anything. He plopped himself down on a stump, which conveniently sits outside the hemp factory that was located at the mouth of the creek. I waited for him to collect himself, trying to look modest, but it was hard. He caught his breath and took a good puff on his cigar. "Well now, tell me all about this, Cal," he urged. "It sounds a mighty fine business, mighty fine."

And so I explained how Andrew Jackson, "Old Hickory" himself, was coming to Lexington for the Fourth of July celebration. I was talking in a big rush and King said he knew about that, everyone did. So I told how Dame Rutledge had to pick someone to sing a patriotic song and how we girls at her school had been having contests all fall and the final contest was just that day and how the someone who won turned out to be me: Calendula Farmer of Second Creek. Recovered from my flash of shyness, I executed a turn and a curtsy. King remained speechless at first, shaking his head in gratifying appreciation of my achievement and gazing at me with soft approving brown eyes.

"Your ma and Aunt Charlotte are up at your house," he told me at last. "I expect they'll be mighty proud to hear your news, young Cal. My, my," he said, shaking his head gently and puffing his cigar. "Why, I'm just about tickled to death over this. I believe I may have to go drink a toast to you, my child. The President of the United States, you said." I nodded eagerly, smiling from cheek to cheek. "Who coulda thunk such a thing? Now this is what I call a real honest to goodness honor." I reveled in his amazement and praise although I tried not to. Taking my arm, he pushed himself up from the stump, tipped his black top hat to me, and shuffled on toward Postlethwait's Tavern to find a citizen soft enough to buy him a drink in my honor.

I did find Aunt Charlotte in our house with Mama and Jackie. And indeed they were happy enough to hear my news and made me sing my song all the way through. But they were happier yet to set me to spinning wool so that Mama could start our supper and Aunt Charlotte could work on making her medicines at the table.

Aunt Charlotte had been born a slave and lived as one for the first twenty or twenty-five years of her life, but when her master died, he set her free. In his will he made out the manumission papers proclaiming her a free black woman, and further deeded to her the house she lives in. He also granted her a license to sell baked goods in town, and the right to have a stall in the covered market. Aunt Charlotte is the only black woman in Lexington who has these privileges. She sometimes wears a headscarf and sometimes does not, even though the law says all black women must keep their heads covered at all times. And even though blacks are not allowed to own a horse or carriage, Aunt Charlotte owns both and drives around town regularly making deliveries and house calls. To my certain knowledge no one has ever challenged her. It's as though she lives between the laws.

Everyone calls her Aunt Charlotte, or sometimes they call her Free Charlotte, but for me, she actually was like my aunt, in a real way. For one thing she birthed me as she never let me forget. "It was the iciest night I ever did see," she would start when she got on that story. As a child I believed she actually blamed me for the weather that night, for I'd often heard her say, when she'd be called out for a birth, a death, or something in between, "Why on earth can't a body wait till it's warmer or drier or later?" She was a reluctant midwife to the slave women in town, but her reputation as a wise woman and a healer was golden among the poor of all colors. Aunt Charlotte and Mama became best friends long ago and she and King have always been family to me. Never more so, nor never so needed, as during that year, 1833.

But on that day in late January when I won the Singing Prize and knew I was to sing before the President, the sun was shining brightly, the future—at least mine—looked rosy. All was right in the world, except for my Pa, who was a perpetual cloud over my life. He had been around less and less since last summer, but it hadn't always been like that. When I was little, there were good times with Mama and Pa and me and all of us smiling or singing and just being happy. I didn't make that up, although sometimes it feels like I must have. It faded away until it was only a memory and a little girl's memory at that. Perhaps I was wrong. Had there always been those blaring silences, those fierce glances, and a live tension in the room as palpable as a coiled snake? Memory is a tricky business, layered as it is by desire, but I really do think, long ago, things were right between my parents.

My mother and father came to Lexington from Boston and Philadelphia respectively. They believed fervently in the new nation. They were actively interested in building a democracy, and perhaps because they were from the North, or perhaps because they could see how wrong it was, they opposed slavery openly. The frontier called to them as far as Lexington where opportunities abounded for my father. He opened the first hemp factory in town, just down the creek from us. He was doing well because everybody needs hemp for just about everything, and here in Kentucky it grows freely and vigorously. Although the work was hard and the hours long, Pa and Mama were thriving. He built our house in 1819. He was proud of his work and it was a good home. He promised to add on but that never happened.

I was the first baby born in Lexington in 1820, "a New Year's baby" they called me in the *Gazette*, the article Mama saved to show me, dry and cracking even back then, now swept away by the flood. Growing up it made me feel a bit like royalty to have gotten noticed in the newspaper just for being born. As I got big enough to help, Mama and I tended the house and garden, the goat and the chickens. We spun and sewed and baked and hoed; we worked hard, but it was a good house and we made a good family back then.

Then in April of 1828 there was a terrible fire at Pa's business. It started by no one knew what, and the factory burned to the ground, and Pa couldn't get over it. Ever. He lost a lot of money, and there was no way to get it back. The hemp factory was completely destroyed and he didn't have what was needed to rebuild. That fire marks the first big crack in our family. From there it spread to full fracture.

Pa went from job to job, but it was always the same: he got into arguments and brawls with the men in charge and soon he was let go because he couldn't get along with anyone. Pa was surly tempered to the point people didn't want to be around him. He didn't used to be that way. He was well liked, in spite of his abolitionist opinions, and he participated in the civic and government life of our city. At one time, Jack Farmer was a respected name in Lexington, and Mama told me once that Pa had been asked to serve as an Alderman. But all that was now long ago and like so much, what was important then, is mere misty history now.

The hemp factory was rebuilt and run by William Clagget and his son James. Life went on. But for us, for Pa, the fire was a wall he could never get past. It was an end for him. He took the fire personally, that God or Fate or something had aimed it at him, and the unfairness of it stopped him in his tracks. His anger was quick and total and all consuming. He lashed out at anyone near over anything. He was mean to Mama and me too, backhanding us both as if we were nothing to him but something in his way. He said hurtful things that even yet echo through my mind on a bad night. Once he started drinking heavily, it got worse in a hurry. After the fire, Mama started working with Aunt Charlotte, and we delivered breads and buns all over town. We took in laundry and sold eggs and managed, but what had been hard became much harder.

Then, Pa got on with the railroad. The plan was to lay track from Lexington all the way to Frankfort. There was money to be made and he went for it. He slept on the site somewhere in between the two cities and ate in the railroad camp. At the beginning of that year, 1833, Pa had been gone for many months and sending money home, which was a good thing because Jackie had been born in September and Mama couldn't do as much as she had before. We didn't see Pa much and we didn't miss him much either. Not the him he'd turned into. I could still—still can—miss the him he used to be. But I was learning there were things I could do nothing about. And bringing Pa back was one of them.

Chapter III

Mama

Even before the flood, I had known it was my last term at school and, in truth, I was glad, because I knew Mama had sold her brooch, the one with the ruby and diamonds. She'd sold it to pay for me to go to school and I often felt guilty and reproached myself when I was cross or bored or frustrated with the slow pace of Dame Rutledge's classroom. Now it seemed a wonder to be able to finish school by performing for the actual President of the United States. He had just been reelected the previous year and although he defeated Lexington's own Henry Clay, it was still an uncommon honor. I intended to make Mama proud, and had spent most of that winter practicing my song. I practiced every verse, trying out a new emphasis here, a pause there. Even though I had been sent to Dame's school, my real learning was done at home.

My mother was a woman uncommonly fond of learning. She was from an old Boston family, the Brights, and one of her ancestors had helped to found Harvard

College. When I was little she taught me how to read and write and how to do arithmetic. She would even let me off of chores sometimes for an hour or so to write in my own private notebook. "You've got to practice it to learn it," she'd tell me. That, and "Think the full of your thoughts." I suppose that is the very basis of Freethinking. Freethinking is not a religion exactly, but it's a commitment nonetheless, to think your own thoughts freely and fully.

Thinking is an odd business in my experience. I used to figure I knew exactly what I thought about something. But then, the more I actually thought about it, the more angles I questioned it from, quite often, instead of getting clearer, things got muddier. This was what my mother referred to as "the full of your thoughts." It is the muck that any open mind must wade through to get to the firmer ground of clarity. I still do not enjoy uncertainty but I have learned to tolerate it as a necessary element of Freethinking.

My mother was raised as a Freethinker by her family in Massachusetts and she was raising me to be a Freethinker too, but here in Kentucky it wasn't a thing highly esteemed. I had long grown used to girls at school who had been told they were not to "know" me; what fools I thought them, letting someone else tell them how to think much less who they know or don't know. When I was young, it hurt my feelings, but by the age of thirteen I was well used to being snubbed for being my mother's daughter. And my father's. And increasingly, at that age, for being myself.

As a Freethinker, Mama was also a free speaker, not hesitating to share her ideas with people, even when they didn't much want to hear it. One summer, the City of Lexington held a special ceremony at the court-house to celebrate our nation's independence. The city had just incorporated and just about everyone who lived anywhere near town packed a lunch and came out to hear the speeches and the music. Henry Clay spoke and Dr. Bainbridge, who is from Transylvania College and famous for inventing something, although I don't remember what. Mr. Hunt spoke too, of course. He was the mayor back then. Musicians were playing banjo and fiddle music and there were mobs of people selling wares from their wagons or even just sitting on the cobblestones.

The courthouse faced Postlethwait's Tavern, which establishment had set out long tables and big tents where they were selling spirits and such. Much laugh-ter came from that side. The courthouse sported a large front lawn with steps leading up to a mezza-nine kind of platform. There, the City Fathers were arranged on a dais overlooking us all. Mama and I had walked up the few blocks from Town Branch with Aunt Charlotte who decided to leave her cart at home in deference to the crowds. I was trying to set a sprightlier pace but they were murmuring in each other's ear and taking their time, making our progress maddeningly slow. We were there, I naively thought, to enjoy the day and hear the speechifying. I should have guessed Mama would do a little speechifying herself.

27

For a long time we stood with the crowd, listening to the esteemed men of our town address us. Then Mama walked forward to the center of the platform where the speakers stood and I knew what she was going to do. My blood began pounding in my head so hard I could barely hear anything else. I followed her and we stood beneath the City Fathers together. Mama stood straight and still, waiting to be recognized. Finally, the Reverend Kinkaid inclined his head.

"Mrs. Farmer, do you have something to say?" he inquired in a patronizing tone. He was a beaky looking man and in his black robes he appeared a veritable buzzard.

"I do," Mama said in a squeaky, scratchy, scared kind of voice. She cleared her throat, shook her head at some internal voice, and took a deep breath. In a lower, stronger key she raised her voice and intoned slowly, "Ladies and gentlemen of Lexington, friends, neighbors, citizens: We are gathered here today to celebrate freedom and American justice, democratic justice." Her voice was strong now and rang out around the plaza; even the patrons of Postlethwait's were leaning forward to hear. "Our nation, the United States of America, stands as a beacon to the world; the American system of jurisprudence stands for justice and justice for all." She paused. "Even slaves." I could feel her arm trembling but her voice was steady and full. The crowd had grown even quieter and a silence fell.

At last one of the City Fathers nodded and said, "A pretty speech, Madam. Where is your husband?" A few snickered and someone in the back made whistling noises that seemed terribly rude. My face was bright red and burning but I stood fast. I couldn't let her do this alone. I loved her loyally as a daughter, and even at that relatively young age I had thought my way through slavery many a time and decided quite independently, or so I thought—as everyone thinks when they come into their own—that slavery was an abomination, a wrong thing, a poison in the country's body that would kill us if we couldn't rid ourselves of it.

"Which is why," Mama continued, raising her voice slightly and ignoring his question, "it is a terrible crime before God to defame these halls of justice with the sin of slave trading. Do not allow the slave market to pollute this sacred ground."

At this point I am not sure exactly what all happened, but there were some jeers from the crowd and someone spit tobacco juice quite close to my feet. I heard some growled cuss words that frightened me, even though I wasn't sure what they meant. Mama stood perfectly erect so I did too. Finally, the moment became uncomfortable, and Mayor Hunt said, with mock civility, "Thank you for your input, Mrs. Farmer. Now perhaps you had best go tend to your home. We will look after the city without your assistance. Somehow," he added as an aside and won the crowd's laughter.

I saw, and I am sure Mama did too, the sheriff approaching. She turned around and we walked slowly away, holding our heads high. As the crowd parted to let us through, Aunt Charlotte joined us and she and my mother walked together the whole way home, again talking softly to each other. I followed behind this time, both glad I didn't have to stay and endure the mocking and teasing I knew would be my fare in the days and weeks and months to come, and mad that I had been denied my day of holiday. I would eat no taffy, nor would I hear any more speeches that day.

I was both appalled and proud of her action, and so of my own. I didn't have to follow her into the middle of the stage, but I did. She had spoken of these views about the courthouse being polluted by the slave trade before, with both me and Aunt Charlotte. I don't know if she knew herself she was going to do what she did that day until she was on her feet and doing it.

Aunt Charlotte fussed at her the rest of that day, but Mama just pursed her lips and kept busy fixing supper and having me chop firewood, draw water, and fetch potatoes from the cellar. But I heard enough of what was said to understand. "Margaret, you need to have a care," Aunt Charlotte said. "They's some mighty powerful men in this town who don't like hearing from an uppity woman, even if she is white. We both know there are others who believe as we do, but Maggie girl, have you noticed? They ain't going 'round drawing all that attention to themselves, now are they?"

"It's wrong," Mama said. "I despise the slave trade and I have to protest it. You know me, Charlotte." Her voice was tired but sharper too than usual.

"They's ways and they's ways of protesting it. You know that too," Aunt Charlotte answered.

30

"Well, this is my way," Mama said.

"Woman, you ever wondered what life would be like if you wasn't making a scandal?"

Mama gave a small smile. "Yes, I've considered it once or twice, but it seemed to me somebody needed to say something."

"And it had to be you, Margaret? You had to be the one to say something?"

There was a long silence and I thought Mama might not answer at all, but she finally said simply, "Yes."

Eventually, Aunt Charlotte shook her head, gave Mama and me her warm if brief embrace and went home. Mama was like that and Aunt Charlotte knew it better than most. Mama thought the full of her thoughts and she spoke the full of her mind and if people thought less of her, that was just the way it was. She had always taught me to care more about the opinion of my own conscience than the opinion of other people. "You are the one who must lie down with yourself at night. A clean conscience is a soft pillow, and it is up to you, daily, Cal, to decide what is right and what is wrong."

Of course Mama's speech never made a dime's worth of difference; the slave market has been held on the courthouse grounds since ever there was a courthouse. In Lexington, there are slave jails under the stores and offices on the streets surrounding the courthouse, including one under Henry Clay's law office on Upper Street. When auction day comes, the old, the young, the sick, and the disabled are herded over to Cheapside for sale at bargain prices.

31

I had only seen the slave market once (and that by mistake). I was delivering a bakery order for Aunt Charlotte and passed by Cheapside without thinking. As I walked, I slowly became aware of a high, terrible keening. Before I registered what the sound was, my blood had chilled and I came out all over in goosebumps. As I kept walking, I saw a bleeding, chained, writhing, and sobbing cluster of brown men, women, and children. The raw anguish rose like a poisonous vapor that engulfed the group and seemed to torture every breath.

Mama had never wanted me to see it, she said, and after that day, I understood why. I ran hard away from that place, but still dreamed afterwards of those dreadful sounds, the sights, and the very atmosphere of despair I had glimpsed. Because both my parents were firm abolitionists, I grew up thinking slavery was wrong. But being a Freethinker I had to eventually work it through for myself. I could see where if I were a slave owner I might think it a good system—lifelong, reproducing free labor trained to know my needs and meet them. But the problem comes when I consider the situation from the side of the slave, being "owned" by someone else, made to do the owner's bidding, humiliated on a whim, and punished for any protest. If I could imagine that the people from Africa were not human, would that make owning them acceptable? It couldn't be done. Aunt Charlotte's beautiful face and warm embracing lap were imprinted in my earliest memories. I loved her. How could I deny her humanity?

After a particularly heated and unusually lively classroom discussion one day, Dame Rutledge ruled that slavery was not a topic for young ladies and thus its further mention was forbidden at school. Everyone knew how I felt and what I thought anyway, and after Mama and I stepped out at the courthouse that day, I imagined the whole town knew how we felt. There were other abolitionists in Lexington, but none as vocal and outspoken as my mother. Mama counseled there was no harm in others knowing how you thought and felt about things. "Keep humble and open minded," she said, "but strive to find what is right and real for you. And when you firmly do believe something and want to talk to others about it, do so. Just be mindful no one is obligated to agree with you, no matter how passionately you feel about your point. There are many ways of thinking and understanding; the same set of facts may prove opposite things to different people, but there is no reason you shouldn't let your voice be heard, Cal."

She was talking to me that time, just before I fell asleep. Her warm fingers were stroking through my hair, gently scratching my scalp. Her voice, soft and lulling, continued, "Some will say because you are a girl and because you are young, you don't deserve to have a voice, but I have known you all your life, daughter, I know the way you think things through. As long as you mind your manners and show real respect to all, there is no reason you should not join the discussion, whatever it may be about."

I knew no other child with a mother as open and interesting as mine. Indeed, I knew few other children well. Once our family fortunes failed and Pa became an angry whirlwind, we were increasingly isolated socially. Beyond a nodding acquaintance with several hundred folk, we really had no circle of friends beyond Aunt Charlotte and King.

Although Mama allowed that I speak my mind, she would also remind me often of the virtues of silence. "Silence is golden," she murmured when I had been prattling on too long. She was also fond of pointing out how God had given us two eyes, two ears, and only one mouth—for a reason that anyone who could count could figure out.

Mama and I lived peacefully and happily without Pa that fall and winter, and although our life was not easy, it was good. My little brother Jackie was a beautiful happy baby and I carried him around with me everywhere. Thus 1833 waltzed in, a deceptively mild-faced year, shot through with optimism. Not only I, but the whole town was excited about the upcoming Fourth of July events. Winning the Singing Prize and the honor that came with it had made my thirteenth year seem my best yet. I looked ahead eagerly, knowing nothing of what was to come.

Chapter IV

Tweeny

The Hunt-Adams house is one of the most beautiful in all of Lexington, which is a town full of beautiful houses. I had seen it many times, passed by it on High Street when making deliveries for Aunt Charlotte, but had never been inside. The house and its grounds, including the slave cabins out back, take up the entire block between High and Upper.

On the first night before following Cook up the stairs, I saw very little. Mrs. Hunt-Adams whisked me out of the front hallway into the kitchen. "Put her to bed and let her sleep in the morning," she instructed Cook as though I were not there. "We'll give her a day to get herself accustomed to us and give you a chance to find provisions for her. Anything else?" She seemed to muse, then said, "Oh, yes, put her in with Mrs. Alice, that should be fine for both of them." With that she swept out and into some other part of the house. I saw her rarely after that; our lives were separate and our paths almost never crossed.

That first night I slept deeply, blankly. I slept in for a few hours the next day and awakened early in the afternoon; awakened with a start of fear. As soon as I awoke, before I even opened my eyes, I knew I wasn't at home, but it was awhile before I was able to track myself down to the fourth floor attic room of the Hunt-Adams house on High Street. And sure enough, there I was.

When I did open my eyes I was surprised by how light it was. There was more light on the fourth floor than there was in our entire house on Second Creek. Being up so high was thrilling. The sun was streaming through the little oval window and spilling onto Mrs. Alice's neatly made up bed. Placed carefully on her bed were clothes I assumed were meant for me. I put on the clean cotton undershift and the brown stuff dress, completely practical and surprisingly well fitting. There were stockings and those same ill-fitting shoes from the night before. I put them on against my better judgment and hobbled down the stairs.

Cook looked up from some chopping she was doing and saw me hobbling. She raised her eyebrows but merely said, "Sit and eat. I'll explain your duties to you." She gave me a bowl of porridge and a glass of milk, which I was grateful for as my stomach had been growling at me since I awoke. As I slowed my eating, she placed a cup of tea in front of me and sat down herself, something I was to learn she seldom did.

"Now, Miss Calendula Farmer, how old did the missus say you were?"

"Thirteen, ma'am," I replied cautiously.

"Thirteen, you say?" She sighed deeply and with evident pleasure. "Now that's what I would call a splendid age for a tweeny."

"A tweeny, ma'am?"

"That's what you've been hired on for; didn't she tell you?"

"She said a maid, ma'am," I said in a soft voice, my spirits growing weak.

"Well, that's one way of putting it, but a tweeny is…" Here she paused and turned her blue eyes on me. "Well, a tweeny is step one to becoming a maid."

I stared at her dumbfounded. Step one? I didn't want to become a maid; I didn't need a step one. "Ma'am?" I stuttered, as politely as I could.

Cook eyed me for a long moment over her teacup then took a deep drink.

"Look here, Missy," she began, setting her cup carefully into its saucer. "A tweeny is the lowest job in this house for a white girl. You're called a tweeny because most of what you do will be between stairs. I'll use you here in the kitchen, Mrs. Alice will use you in the basement with the laundry, and you'll be sent to do different chores under Miss Ingram's direction. She is the Housekeeper, I am the Cook. You address me as Cook and, so far, you're doing just fine on the ma'ams." To my amazement—and to this day I doubt my perceptions—she winked at me. I took heart.

"You will take your orders from me. Today is a free day for you to adjust, I believe the missus said. So I say, get to know the layout of the back stairs and the rooms immediately off of them. That, besides the kitchen and the laundry, will be your responsibility. Hmm," Cook scratched at her chin as if she had whiskers. "Take your shoes out to Lawton in the barn and have him slit them so you can wear those until we find you something better. I need you on your feet."

"Yes, ma'am."

"Now, what else do you want to know?"

I considered. I had so many questions but I sensed my time with her was short. "What are my duties?" I ventured.

"Your duties are whatever I say they are," she said. "Understand?"

"Yes, ma'am, I do."

She made a move to rise from the table and before she could leave I asked, "Who all lives here?"

Cook continued pushing up and away from the table, but she answered me, "It's none of your concern, Calendula Farmer. And that name, by the way, is a mouthful; what do people call you?"

"Cal," I replied, barely able to meet her gaze.

"Now then, Cal, who lives here is none of your business. You are a tweeny, an employee who was hired and who can be fired just as quickly. Do you understand me?" She glared at me from where she stood above me and, meekly, I answered yes.

Apparently mollified, Cook proceeded to tell me who lived there and where. "There are three children, lovely young people." She looked at me and seemed to imply I could learn from their superior example.

"Amelia is ten, Jack, eight, and Anna is the baby; she's only two. There is also the Nanny Bell and the Governess, Miss Ethridge. They, along with myself, have lodgings in the West Wing. There is a school room there, which you will be responsible for cleaning. Then, there is also Mrs. Bell, the missus's mother, who lives in the East Wing, along with Mrs. Hunt-Adams's companion and secretary, Miss Wilder. This is of interest to you, uh…" she searched her brain and found my name, "… Cal—only because you will be cleaning their quarters from time to time, emptying chamber pots if Missy or one of the other girls takes sick, and doing occasional odd jobs as I command."

That first day, however, after Cook had answered what questions I had that she deemed acceptable, I was free to wander and observe (as long as I did not go into the main rooms of the house: the reception hall, the meeting rooms, the parlors, the music room, the library, the second floor bedrooms, the nursery, plus who knows whatever other rooms—these were completely forbidden me). Cook drew my boundaries, made sure I understood she meant business, and set me free, so explore I did, what was allowed to me.

Off the back stairs at the level of the kitchen was a room used as a larder, a supply house where Cook kept hams and bins of flour and all manner of things. In the basement, which had six oversized limestone cavernous rooms, every one of them bigger than our house on Second Creek, I found the ironing board, which would keep me company for many hours in my near future. At the furthest end of the furthest room, I found Mrs. Alice who was overseeing two women who were stirring huge vats of boiling clothes. She saw me and turned to me. I remember what Cook said about her not being much of a conversationalist, but I introduced myself anyway.

"Hello, I'm Cal Farmer, the new tweeny," I said, trying out the word.

She gave me an amused look and finally blinked her eyes at me which seemed to mean she'd heard me. Mrs. Alice was maybe forty or fifty or maybe sixty. It's hard to tell with some people and she was one of them. She was a slim, neat woman with a heart-shaped face and soft hazel eyes. She wore a bleached white shift over a plain stuff dress, much like my own. Her hair was pinned in a tight bun and looked to be mostly gray. I never learned if Alice was her first or second name. Everyone called her Mrs. Alice so I did too. And I never learned if her silence was by choice or necessity. It too was simply accepted, so I accepted it too. I was to spend many hours in Mrs. Alice's quiet company, and came to know her as a silent but friendly companion.

The back stairs on the second floor passed by a mop room, with brushes and mops and rags and buckets and some gadgets I didn't even know the names for. Beyond that were the family's rooms, the nursery, and the wing where the governess lived as did the nurse. I peered out into the great hall laid with a Turkish carpet, or I think that is what it's called. Quickly, I ducked back, afraid to lose my job on the first day.

Missy and Georgia, another slave girl who lived on the property, worked as indoor maids, and both confirmed for me what Cook had told me: the tweeny gets the roughest jobs there are. They felt superior to me and although they were not really rude I could tell they enjoyed passing me on the steps as they tripped up, giggling, to work in the upstairs rooms.

Perhaps it is our nature to want someone lower than us, sad if you think about it. The one good thing about not being allowed on the second floor was that I didn't have to empty all those chamber pots. I only had to do Mrs. Alice's and mine, plus Cook's and Mrs. Ingram's, whose quarters were in yet another wing that led off through the kitchen.

At the top of the stairs, I discovered that there was not only our room, which was the first room to the left, but a warren of little rooms led off the long winding hallways that stretched the length of the house. The peak in our room was only one dormer of many. Cook explained they were used for visiting maids who come with guests. When I went outside that day, and craned my neck to see the top, I confirmed my suspicion; there was more to this vast house than I could discover in a day. Not to mention the places I had been explicitly barred from exploring.

The slave cabins, however, were perfectly easy to visit as they were just down the lane off the kitchen garden. There were two cabins, and I wandered into the cleared dusty space in front of them. Suddenly two little boys came darting out of one of the cabins and stopped dead in their tracks when they saw me. They looked nearly scared to death. I smiled and stopped walking. In fact, I stood very still. They turned and ran inside yelling, "Mama!" That is how I met Jimmy. She squinted at me hard when I introduced myself and said, "You any kin to that Farmer lady stood up on Independence Day?" When I told her I was her daughter, she invited me in. She had already heard about the flood and was never gladder they lived up high. While we talked, the little boys, Bud and Billy I learned they were, ran in and out of the cabin.

Jimmy was their mother and the mother of two more: Eli, her oldest, worked in the stables, and Georgia, who I'd already met, worked in the house for Mrs. Ingram. Jimmy's husband, Thomas, had been born to this family she told me. "We been with these folks many years," she said. "In fact, Lawton, you met him?" I nodded. "He lives next door with Missy, his granddaughter. Lawton was born in Virginia before the Hunt-Adamses ever came out west to here," she explained.

"Jimmy?" I ventured.

"Yes?"

"How come they have two last names? I never knew anyone like that before." This question had been burning in me since I was first introduced to Mrs. Hunt-Adams, but I couldn't imagine asking Cook, much less the lady herself. But it seemed odd to me and unwieldy.

Jimmy laughed. "Well, that story goes way back before my time or even Lawton's. They was two mighty powerful families and when the young people went to get married, neither family would let go of its name. So instead of the girl taking the boy's name, they merged their names and it's been that ever since."

I thought about this. "So Mrs. Hunt-Adams wasn't Miss Hunt?"

"Law no, she was a Bell, from right here in town."

"But what if her family wanted to keep their name too? Would she be Mrs. Bell-Hunt-Adams?"

We both laughed at that and started putting names together to be funny. Jimmy was the warmest person I'd met here. She was the seamstress for the family and had made the dress I wore. She had to get back to work so I left reluctantly, but she called after me, "Don't you be a stranger, Miss Calendula Farmer!"

What I wanted to do was run home and see Mama. I was desperately curious about our house, but I had been told not to leave the grounds. I was too obedient to even consider defying that order. It was a strange feeling to be so divided. Part of me was fascinated with this new house, riveted to the sights and sounds, the new people, the beauty and spaciousness and grandeur of it all, but another part—for once something rivaled my curiosity—was absolutely focused on Second Creek and the people there. What had happened? What was left? And too, had Mama really meant to send me up here? Perhaps today she was regretting her choice and just waiting for me to turn up.

I knew that wasn't so, but for a while the fantasy comforted me. That first day as a tweeny, that day hung suspended between what was and what is, between yesterday and today, between when I lived at home and when I lived away and made a salary.

The very word salary repeated in my head like a bell. Earning a wage, a salary. We learned last year the very word comes from *sal*, meaning salt in the earliest Latin. Paid in salt, those soldiers marched on, doing as they were bid, the will of the Roman Empire. And I was paid in coin to do Cook's bidding. At some point during that strange day, I simply accepted the split and imagined myself with a line down the middle: one side green with the newness and the other side blue with longing.

I never saw the family that day and in fact had very little to do with any of them ever. They literally lived in a different world, on the other side of the doors that separated my world from theirs. I would sometimes hear the children's voices raised in play as they frolicked in some game, but I was never to meet them.

I never met Mr. Hunt-Adams but once and that only to be formally introduced to him. He was a short stout man with a rapidly balding top. He eyed me over his spectacles and said he would expect my best service. I curtsied and mumbled agreement, and that was that.

Even Mrs. Hunt-Adams was only occasionally seen on our side of the kitchen door. The only time I saw everyone who lived there was on Sunday morning when we all gathered in the front hall, the slaves and I in the back. The master would lead us in prayer and enjoin us to work hard and be good. It was during these times I saw with little peeks from lowered eyes the rest of the household.

As it turned out, Cook kept me gainfully employed my every waking hour. And whatever housekeeping tasks I undertook, bringing in wood and kindling, cleaning the hallways and always, always, the stairs, the back stairs were my kingdom. I mopped them, scrubbed them, up and down, all four floors, from attic to the basement, countless times. Every day I was on my knees cleaning those stairs. And they were filthy every time I bent to my task. All the slaves and servants running up and down managed to keep them in regular need of my rags and brushes. Not to mention the spills from the chamber pots.

At first the shock of how changed my life had become overwhelmed me, seriously overwhelmed me, to the point that sometimes I would have dizzy spells just thinking about all the changes. Cook was the one who ordered my days, from predawn cleaning grates and setting the fires until long past dusk when I helped in the kitchen wiping dishes. My chores were hard but only on my body. Being a tweeny is a hard life: no one wanted my life, including me, but I was lucky to get it.

Each night at bedtime, I looked out the little window in my room. Just down the hill, only a few minutes' walk, were Mama and Jackie and Aunt Charlotte. How were they? I could feel my heart thudding. On tiptoes I strained vainly to see even a glimpse of something I could pretend was Second Creek, but the angle of the window was wrong. Instead, I blew a kiss to float down and land on them.

Chapter V

My First Visit Home

In all honesty, I have very limited memory of the next few weeks. I worked constantly, harder than I had ever worked before in my life, and looking back I can recall only a dull insistent ache that never left and a haze of consciousness as I moved endlessly from one menial job to another.

I awoke before anyone else to make the fires in the predawn chill. I crept downstairs and swept and built the kitchen fire as well as three fires in the basement. Once the fires were roaring, which was not always an easy feat to accomplish, I hauled water to heat for Cook. In March, it was still freezing early in the morning and many times I had to break the surface on the well.

Once Cook took her place in her kitchen, the pace of my job intensified. For I was Cook's helper, and whether it was stirring porridge, beating eggs, cutting up fruit, turning pancakes, running out to the chicken coop for eggs or maybe to the barn for extra milk, I

47

was kept busy, always. There was no time to stop, to think, to gaze, to wonder.

Always, after breakfast had been served to the family and I had done the dishes—a task that took a good deal of time what with heating the water and then drying and putting the dishes away—my next job was the stairs. From attic to basement, I was in charge of cleaning them every day. First I swept them to gather any dust, and then washed them with scrub bucket, brush, and rag. By the time I finished, it was time to help Cook with the midday meal and by the time that was over I was sent to the basement to help Mrs. Alice. Mostly she had me wringing sheets, huge wet loads of laundry that strained my already aching back. We had so many sheets from all the beds in the mansion, it seemed a mountain. At home, helping Mama, I had learned to wash and wring, but laundry for a small family is nothing at all compared to the army we seemed to be washing for in that house.

Sometimes I would see Jimmy in the basement. She had a room of her own, one in which I built a fire every morning, a sewing room with a mannequin and a long table for measuring and cutting. We neither of us had time to talk, but it was still always good to see a friendly face. There were little basement windows so the gray limestone walls were always dimly lit during the day. Toward the end of March we had a long rainy spell and I felt always as if I were walking through a fog.

At first, I remember thinking I would die. I worked so hard and ached so badly I didn't know how I could go on. After that, I sometimes wished I would die just so I could quit working. The only good thing I can say about that early period is that exhaustion is a wonderful cure for not being able to sleep. Or perhaps it was the Hunt-Adams house, but I slept as I had rarely, if ever, slept before. I would lie down and a few pictures would flash before me, pictures of the day, maybe bits of conversations and that would be all. Before I could go into the serious worrying and brooding that used to plague my nights, I was pulled under and asleep.

At the end of the first week I was given a dollar, and a half day off to finally go see Mama and Jackie and everyone up Second Creek. I hurried along the streets and broke into a run when I got on the last path. Mama was sitting in her rocker—it survived!—nursing Jackie and her face melted into a warm and welcoming smile when she saw me.

"Oh, Mama, I have missed you so much," I said, which was true but not something I allowed myself to dwell on, for fear of becoming melancholy.

"Aye, daughter, and I, you," she replied. "Your brother isn't nearly the conversationalist you are, although he does run on."

Just then, Jackie, hearing my voice, pulled away from Mama and beamed at me. We both laughed.

"So tell me everything," Mama and I both said at the same time and laughed again.

"Would you take time for a cup of tea?" I asked, and when she assented, I went to the stove to check the kettle and prepare our mugs. Looking around, I saw

49

there was less in the house than there had been. The bed was there, but new straw stuffed a new mattress and it was much thinner than it had been.

The part of the room where I usually slept still held a chest, but there was nothing in it. "I'm afraid your diary was destroyed," Mama said when she saw me looking in that corner. The kitchen table stood strong, but there were only two chairs now, and I found only two cups, not the six we had before. The book shelf, Mama's prize possession, which used to hold our collection of the family Bible, Shakespeare's sonnets, and her few treasured novels, stood empty. I knew without asking how much that hurt.

The house smelled strongly of old mud, and soap. It was as though the odors were warring with each other for dominance. Mama had clearly been spending her time doing much the same as I had—scrubbing. But while I worked on those blasted back stairs, she worked on home. She told me Miss Em had floated away, but that there had come a new goat that had wandered in or floated down from somewhere upstream. She named her Nanny and said it was a miracle that Nanny was giving milk.

I told her about Cook and Mrs. Alice and Jimmy, Georgia and Missy and Lawton, and how I never saw any of the family, although I could hear them. I told her the house actually had four levels, if she could believe it. I barely could and I lived there. "When you look out the window in my room, you can see all the way to Transylvania and that big new building named for Captain Morrison. I can see even farther than that but there isn't much to see. It's a tremendous feeling, Mama, to be standing so high above everything."

Mama nodded and listened and sipped her tea and put Jackie on the floor to play. "Yes, our house in Boston had four floors too, but it wasn't quite so grand as where you are now, but I know what you mean about being up high. Tell me about your studies, Cal, what are you learning?"

I looked down for I could never lie to Mama, try though I might. "I've been so tired, Mama," I started, and then said, "I haven't had the time or the energy."

"What? You are to be given the time; remember, it was discussed." I admitted that Cook had given me an hour this week, but I had fallen asleep. Mama's eyes, so sad already, seemed to get a little sadder. She said, "As for the energy, that will improve as you accustom yourself to the work."

"I can only hope so, Mama. I have never been so tired in all my life."

She eyed me critically and said, "I think you've grown. Is that even possible?" In truth, I'd been wondering the same thing. My dress pulled tighter around my shoulders. "And look at your arms!" She stopped. "Muscles," she finished weakly, somehow making it sound very unfortunate.

I looked closer at Mama then and noticed she had lost weight. Her smile was ready but thin. She seemed very tired and looked drained. Dark circles blossomed under her eyes and I could feel her trying to hide behind a mask of cheer. She could pretend this was simply an ordinary visit from her daughter who was out making a living, but there was nothing ordinary in our lives any longer. We had all been thrust, rudely and without warning or permission, into circumstances much harder than the hardships we'd experienced previously. When I gave Mama the dollar, however, and saw the naked relief on her face, I felt ashamed of myself for complaining about the work.

We ate dried apples with our tea and slices of bread but there was no butter. As shadows began to lengthen, we both knew I had to leave. I felt hot prickly tears surge up behind my eyes and picked up Jackie to divert myself. He had been babbling happily all afternoon, and if he wasn't the conversationalist I was, he gave every indication he would be soon. Mama came up to me as I was putting on my cloak and hugged me from behind. I stood still and soaked in the good feeling of her arms around me and her head buried in my neck, then turned so I could hug her back. I did cry some on the way back up to the Hill, but had regained my composure by the time I was walking up Upper.

Lawton saw me and pulled the cart he was driving over. "Hop in, Cal, I'll give you a ride home. And don't I have a story to tell." I thanked him and climbed in and proceeded to hear the story that was the talk of the town for weeks after. King had been found drunk and asleep on the street one time too many. The Town Fathers were tired of having an old drunk as the only tenant for their brand new jail so the city put King up for auction. Nine months indentured labor to the highest bidder. "And just you guess who that was? Who was the highest bidder. Come on, now, guess." I stared at him clueless. "Aunt Charlotte!" he burst out and doubled over laughing until a coughing fit took him and by then we were at the stable gate.

"Aunt Charlotte?" I asked when he could talk again.

"Yes, law, ain't that one for the books? And guess what that woman paid for him? Come on now, guess. Guess, Cal, I dare you." He was climbing out of the cart and leading the horse to the trough.

I had no idea how much a man like King's indentured labor would bring. So instead I said, "No, you tell me. I can't imagine."

Luckily Lawton's main delight was in the telling so he went on with good humor. "Now this here is the best part. Eighteen cents. Did you hear me right? Yes, eighteen cents Aunt Charlotte give for King and he is hers now for nine whole months. Can you believe it?"

Frankly, I hardly could, but it turned out to be completely true. No one wanted old King, not even for eighteen cents, but Aunt Charlotte, who surely bought him as much out of friendship as wanting a bargain on a live-in handy man. "What about Aunt Charlotte being a freed slave?" I asked before I thought it might be offensive to ask such a thing of an unfreed slave. But if it was, Lawton gave no indication. He was literally twittering with amusement.

"Hee, hee, hee. Why, it's just like everything else with that woman." (He pronounced it "woe-man.")

"Somehow they just look the other way when it comes to her. Hee hee, what a woman she is."

Shaking my head in bemusement and thanking him for the lift, I went back into the warm aromas and friendly bustle of Cook's kitchen. Honestly, I am ashamed to admit it but I thought Lawton had surely gotten the story upside down somehow. I couldn't imagine what had happened but I doubted it was as he said. It was a good story, for certain, a free black woman buys the labor of a white man and I didn't begrudge Lawton the evident pleasure he derived from imagining it. What I wasn't prepared for was that it was the straight up truth.

This same news had already reached Cook's kitchen from Mrs. Ingram, an undeniably reliable source. Missy came in and soon confirmed it to me when I asked. "Good one, don't you think?" she said, and I smiled but couldn't think of anything to say. I kept thinking of King and imagining how miserable he would be cooped up at Aunt Charlotte's with no whiskey and probably no cigars. I had grown up on the receiving end of Aunt Charlotte's strengthening teas and potions, and I did not envy King the "spring cleaning" he was bound to be undergoing.

Chapter VI

Something Daring

A s the weeks passed, I began doing something daring, something I had been expressly forbidden to do. It felt a little thrilling because I so rarely disobeyed. I was the first one up in the household, the one who stoked the fires and hauled the first water, and during that first hour, I was completely alone. One morning, trudging down the cold attic steps, I saw when I got to the main level that the door between the kitchen and the rest of the house had been left open. I peered into the hallway and then beyond that into a massive room, which just the night before had hosted a full crowd. This was not the dining room, with which I was familiar, having been set to sweeping and mopping it before bed along, of course, with the kitchen. No, this was the parlor or the study or the sitting room or one of the many rooms that had names I didn't understand. And there, in a bronze spittoon, which was halfway filled with sand, lay a large cigar stub.

Looking around and listening closely but hearing no one, I dashed in, fished the stub from the sand and wrapped it in a scrap of newspaper I found in the kitchen. Pocketing it and allowing the guilty thrill of disobedience to wash through me, I was elated at the thought of a gift for King. The Hunt-Adamses had so much and a used cigar stub seemed a small enough thing to have stolen, but still Mama's dictum about a clean conscience being a soft pillow proved true. That night, exhausted as I was, I could not sleep until I had resolved what it was that nagged at me so uncomfortably.

Upon examination I found I wasn't worried so much about stealing a cigar stub, especially since it would soon go into the rubbish if not my pocket, and besides it was for a friend and could even be conceived of—using a rather liberal interpretation—as a gesture of charity. No, what kept me up was that I had defied Cook's orders. As the weeks spun out in my new life, I began to like and respect Cook more and more. She had a temper and could snap and snarl, but she mostly ran an efficient and even friendly kitchen. She ordered me around all day, but in a mannerly way. "Cal, please go fetch ten pounds of potatoes from the storeroom and peel them." She didn't have to say please but she nearly always did. I noticed she said please to Missy and Georgia, and to the other slave women owned by the Hunt-Adamses but housed elsewhere who came in to work. Some of this numerous workforce was in and out of the kitchen every day and especially when the family entertained, which was remarkably often.

Mama had been convinced that manners were the oil that greased the gears of human relations. She insisted that I stand up when any elder—black or white—came into the room, that I wait to eat until given permission by my host or hostess, that I watch for older people and children when on the streets and make certain not to plow them over in my exuberance or hurry. I was taught to chew with my mouth closed and, since before I can remember, to never interrupt when two adults were talking. I learned to say please and thank you just after the word Mama.

"If you can eat," Mama would say, "you can express thanks if there's someone other than you providing it, and if not, then at least thank the good Lord. Practice being grateful and you'll be surprised by how much nicer people seem. Try it, daughter, and see what you think."

"Hmm," I might say.

"Manners are about being kind to and considerate of the people around you. It is your attempt to put others at ease. You do want other people to feel comfortable when they're around you, don't you, Cal?"

"Hmm, yes, I guess." In fact I hadn't thought much about it, but that was exactly what she wanted me to do: think about someone other than myself.

Once I remember her telling me, "It's not that you shouldn't think about yourself, you should. If things are not working for you, you won't be of much good to anyone else. But it's natural, even instinctive to think of yourself. It's difficult at times to think of others, but,"

57

and her eyes would light up with excitement, "it's the key to a fair and just society. The absolute key and it's something everyone, rich and poor, black and white, young and old, why it's something we all can do daily to make the world a better place." Such were the conversations of my childhood.

Cook's gentle manners had impressed me and slowly, in spite of her mealtime tempers, she and I became, well, not friends, but friendly. Sometimes I would say something that would make her smile, and very occasionally she would say something funny. One day she called me in, having heard me being snippy with Deedee, a house slave who sometimes got on my last nerve with her slowness.

"Here, Cal," Cook said, "come get your temper out and beat these eggs within an inch of their lives." Sometimes if I was being too talkative, she'd tell me to put my hot air to good use and blow on the fire. Anyway, upon analysis, after I took the cigar stub, it became clear to me that what bothered me was disobeying Cook.

This is the life of a Freethinker, always thinking. At any rate, after understanding what the problem was, I struggled for a solution. The honorable thing to do would be to ask Cook for permission to forage very carefully into the family rooms after a party and collect cigar stubs for a friend. I wondered if I would have the nerve. But I eventually fell asleep, assuring myself I would ask her next day.

Of course, I never did. It was a small enough crime and I was able to bear its weight on my conscience without losing too much sleep. After all, it was only cigar stubs. And truly, after King was in service to Aunt Charlotte, he was in need of a little comfort. I saw him my next trip home and he did indeed look miserable. King, who was so gentle and good natured when he'd had something to drink, could be downright tetchy sober. So when I secretly handed over my gift of three stubs, and he realized what they were, his face softened into the old smile I'd grown up with.

Aunt Charlotte was working King hard. He had repaired her front steps and was hard at work now on a shed where he would sleep. She had plans for having him build her a separate kitchen for her shop so as not to keep her house so hot in the summer. Oh, she had lots of plans for him and he knew it well. He was one glum old man when I saw him that day in April, sober as Sunday morning and glum as a man can be when held against his will, even by a friend like Aunt Charlotte. I couldn't help him with the whiskey, but my offering seemed to cheer him immeasurably.

April in Kentucky is a kind of paradise. The fields and hedgerows, everything everywhere bursts into extravagant flower and this year was no exception. The grounds of the mansion were ablaze with the purple of the money plant, the lunaria, and all manner of dogwoods and redbud trees, not to mention the cheerful little violets and forget-me-nots. Mrs. Hunt-Adams had planted some narcissi bulbs and tulips and their bright cheerful faces greeted me as I emptied slop buckets, or ran other errands as directed.

Sometime in April, I began to "wake up," that is to recover somewhat from the pace of the work and the shock of sudden change. I began to feel rested and excited again about the day when I awoke before the dawn. I was not eager to leave the warmth of my quilt, but I was finally ready and able. I took my Wednesday afternoon hour to read or write, for along with her promise to give me time, Mrs. Hunt-Adams had also promised to provide me with improving literature and paper. I was still beat like a drum by nightfall and sometimes literally climbed into my bed, but as the days lengthened, so did my strength and stamina. I mostly read works by Thomas Jefferson, which were certainly improving, if a bit long winded (in my humble and truly unqualified opinion).

Jimmy's husband Thomas, along with Eli and their other son, Matthew, managed not only the barn but the kitchen garden. Thomas and Cook, with me to do their bidding, grew all manner of greens and herbs. It was good to work outside and often that April when I got to see Mama I would work her little patch as well, planting potatoes and peas, beans, beets and, ugh, turnips, not to mention all manner of things I've forgotten to mention like carrots and a new root we were trying called "celery."

I was eager to help provide for both Mama and my baby brother. Often, while I worked planting, digging

60

or weeding, King would come by to help me with the heaviest digging, and to answer any questions I had. He was knowledgeable about growing things and I for one took the time to listen to what he had to say. We formed a good team, if only for half a day a week, and sometimes less, depending on his schedule or mine. All of which is to say I did not ever ask Cook if I could help myself to the cigar stubs; I just did it anyway and managed my conscience and my pillow myself. I recognize now this is exactly the kind of compromise most people make with themselves to endure the pangs of guilt that accompany a wrong action.

One morning, Cook called me into the kitchen, where King sat, waiting for me. She set cups of tea in front of us both, and left us at the table.

King looked at me somberly. "I'm here on an errand from your ma," he said. "She wanted you to know as soon as we did."

"Know what?" I asked, although in that very instant I knew myself. "Pa?" I asked and King nodded.

"Honey," he said, then stared at his feet. "I wish I wasn't the one to tell you this, but your pa was killed in a knife fight. Seems like he got talking his Abolition talk and one of them roust-a-bouts took issue and came after him with a knife." King coughed and looked over his shoulder. "Honey bunch, I heard he died easy. Fact, way I heard it, he was asleep when he died." I imagined Pa asleep but more likely passed out drunk as the life ebbed out of him.

"Funeral?" I managed.

King looked down. "Well, actually, sweetie, he was in such bad condition, and . . ." He coughed into his sleeve. "Well, did I mention he killed the other man too? The bodies were in right horrible condition, so they was both put into a pauper's grave in a place outside Frankfort. Your ma says to tell you we'll all go there first chance we get and say a proper goodbye."

A proper goodbye? It would have been nice if Pa had done the same for us. And what of his pay packet, where had all the money gone? Surely he'd saved some for us, hadn't he? Such were the thoughts that first flared in my mind but for once I kept them inside.

Instead, I didn't say anything, I felt a heavy curtain of numbness descend upon me like a cloak, weighing me down but protecting me too. I knew I would live inside it until, in my own time and my own way, I integrated this news into myself. For now, I could only thank King for coming to tell me. He enfolded me in a hug and whispered into my hair, "It's a hard blow, Cal, and I'm awful sorry. You take care, girl, you take care."

I didn't really feel his concern and care, not then, but I knew it was genuine and knew, too, that when I could feel again, it would comfort me. My eyes were dry, although King's were gently weeping as he shuffled out the back door and down the hill. I washed our mugs at the sink. When Cook came back in from wherever she'd been, she looked at me, but said nothing.

"My pa died," I said, wondering if she already knew.

"I know, dear. Mr. Solomon told me. You have my condolences." Her voice was softer than usual.

"Thank you," I mumbled, drying our mugs and putting them back in the cupboard. I couldn't meet her eyes for fear of crying hard and losing my self-control completely. Instead I focused on her calling King "Mr. Solomon" and had to work not to burst out laughing. She said nothing more and I went back to my stairs, blankly working through the hours.

How can you miss what you haven't had in so long? Much longer ago than the months since we'd seen him were the good years for us as a family. I'd been missing my Pa ever since the hemp factory burned down when I was eight. I didn't know what or how to feel about his death and poured myself into the job at hand, whatever it was, instead of thinking.

Thus, in an endless whirl of work and wages and going home when I could, and studying what little I managed, getting slowly and tentatively accustomed to this new life, April passed.

Chapter VII

A Spring Surprise

One day in early May, Cook called me into her kitchen and told me to sit. "Now then, Cal, every year, the family, and I with them," she said this last part with a bit of smugness, "travel back to our old homeplace in Richmond, Virginia. It's a long way and we'll be gone a month."

"A month?" I said in surprise.

"Well, it could be six weeks, depending on the roads. It's a very long way. The point is, you and Mrs. Alice are going to be the only servants left in the house and that's a big responsibility. I expect you to act as if I'm right here, watching you. Do you understand?"

"Ma'am, everyone goes?"

"That's right, except for Mrs. Ingram. She takes this as her chance to stay with her family in Frankfort."

"All the slaves too?"

"That's right, except for Jimmy's Eli. He moves in with some friends in town but he'll be here most days to keep up the gardens. Mrs. Alice uses this as a chance to wash and iron all the linens and curtains and you will be helping her."

I had never heard of something like this, just picking up and moving house for a month or more every year. Mrs. Alice accepted all this with her usual quiet equanimity; she had been through it before. As for me, I wondered if I could go home. I knew Mama would miss the money I was earning but I thought perhaps I could make it up to her by being extra helpful. But Cook and Mrs. Hunt-Adams had other plans for me. Along with helping Mrs. Alice, I would be in charge of the chickens and most astounding of all I was to be trusted with a duster and with keeping the downstairs public rooms tidy. Finally, I would be able to explore those rooms, which I had only glimpsed in stolen moments and wondered about from the other side of the door.

I had never heard of giving rooms names: library, parlor, sun room, breakfast room, sitting room, music room, and dining room. Cook talked to me a very long time, outlining my duties as well as things to be watchful of. The night before they left, Cook told me I could take one whole day off every week, but no more, and did I understand? She locked me in her gaze to make it clear she meant what she said. I was to be a good girl and behave myself. "Yes, ma'am," I reassured her, over and over, thinking I would need to be careful not to break anything. I was fairly fumble fingered in those days and there were times that I have to admit I was undeniably clumsy.

That night I lay awake and watched the full moon traverse the sky outside my oval window. I felt I was on the brink of another new and important phase in my life, as indeed I was. What I could not know, could neither sense nor guess, was the enormous tragedy that loomed on the horizon.

May exceeded April in beauty. I've often wondered since that spring whether things simply look better from up on the Hill than down on Second Creek. Or perhaps, and maybe more likely, I was having my eyes opened to so many new sights and sounds that I looked anew on the simple joys I had begun to take for granted. Like the blooming of the forsythia bushes, dogwood trees, tulips and narcissi as they set the place ablaze that spring with their bright colors. As the weather warmed, I often left open the doors to allow the sweet breezes to waft through the mansion. The freedom I had been given was exhilarating, and at times I sizzled with urges to take advantage of my situation, but I was obedient and minded Cook's orders to take only one day a week to visit Mama and Jackie.

Once, while cleaning the room called the sun room, I found a newspaper from sometime in April. My eye was caught by the horrible headline: "5000 Die in New York City of Cholera." Five thousand people? Surely that couldn't be, but on reading the article I found in fact it was. Five thousand was about the size of Lexington: all those people dead? Cholera had been spreading mysteriously throughout the world for over a year. It was a dreaded disease that killed quickly and with great suffering; the victims were emptied rapidly of all their fluids and died—shriveled, exhausted, and filthy. No one seemed to know what caused cholera but there were many theories. One of the most popular (or was it perhaps merely most vocal?) was that cholera was God's vengeance against his sinful people. Other learned men posited that the disease was carried in the air, a miasma that poisoned all who breathed it. I worried and wondered about this until the next time I was able to see Mama.

Aunt Charlotte and King were at Mama's house the day I visited her. It felt good to be home with all the people I loved best in the world. Jackie had begun to pull himself up and was trying to walk, even though he wasn't yet a year old. We watched him lurch from person to person, his mouth pursed in concentration as he drunkenly wove his way around the house, his little hands grasping a wooden spoon in one and a rag doll in the other, landing often on his rump, to our claps and calls of encouragement. He looked so proud of himself, even sitting on the floor after a fall, just full of smiles and chuckles as he began to sense the huge opportunities in store for him as he transitioned from crawling to toddling. Jackie was a beautiful baby whose golden curls tumbled around his sweet face, a face so often wreathed in smiles and babbling always with news he was anxious to share.

I told them about the newspaper article I'd seen and asked them about cholera. Aunt Charlotte was deathly afraid of it. She had seen it go through the slave quarters when she lived back in Virginia and shuddered as she recalled how quickly it moved. "Like the angel of death, just mowing them down," she said. "Some folk survived, but not most. They could be well in the morning and just gone by night."

"Why didn't you get it?" I asked.

"I have no idea. The good Lord was looking after me as He always has," she said. There was a smugness in her tone that bothered me. Was she more worthy of life than those who had died? I always have this problem when people claim God was looking after them especially. I've never dared to think I understand God—how could I? But there were quite a few questions I would have liked to ask Him, and this being the main one: why do some people suffer so and some live in such ease? I had long ago determined that fortune and misfortune did not seem to visit people based on their evident goodness or badness. So what were the criteria God used to make His judgments? I'd like to know. I saw Mama catch my eye, and I knew she knew what I was thinking. (She knew me so well.) She gave me a small grin and slight shake of her head, warning me not to go further with this.

King told us about an advertisement he'd seen in the paper promising its subscribers wouldn't catch the cholera. He laughed and shook his head. "It was bad down in New Orleans, I'd heard that, but I don't think we have to worry up here," he said.

"Why not?" I asked.

"Why, honey, we're up on a plateau here," King said.

"Lexington is perfectly situated. We got good breezes, plenty good soil for farming, those rolling hills…why this is the finest place in the world." He turned then to a subject never far from his heart. "Yes ma'am, this land is a Paradise. The tobacco grows right up, just begging to be smoked, and Lord a mercy, it's a known fact that Kentucky has the best whiskey made here in these United States."

This earned him a dark look from Aunt Charlotte, but King continued blithely. "And that is also why we raise the finest, fastest race horses in the world right here." He looked at us expectantly, confident he'd made his point, but just in case we'd missed it, he concluded, "I don't think that ole cholera would stand a chance around here. Why last year we only had— what—two deaths out of this whole town. Cholera just can't get a footing here; it's too beautiful."

I had heard that argument before, that Lexington was so perfectly situated that we were protected from the perils and poisons of larger cities. Our courthouse was an imposing and beautiful building. We had a bustling marketplace and Morton's Row, the mercantile building downtown, which had just been built. New houses, certainly not all as grand as the Hunt-Adams's but some even grander, were being built every day. We were a prosperous city and proud of ourselves. And in fact, there was an emphasis on grace and beauty and culture. It's hard to pin such a thing down, but the city itself tried to be grand. We had a French chef who had recently opened an eating establishment, architects designed beautiful estate houses like the mansion I now lived in, and even the smaller buildings were made with an eye to charm and balance and grace. Not so much down on Second Creek where we were our own architects, but certainly up on the Hill.

Mama took the subject back to cholera, my original question, and answered me in the rational, informed, and calm manner she addressed most problems with. "Cal, do you remember Dr. Drake?"

I nodded. He was a famous doctor who taught at the university, but we knew him from having gone to him once when Jackie had a choking spell. He was kind and charitable and when we told him Aunt Charlotte had sent us, he shepherded us into his house and took over the baby's care, curing him within hours.

"Last year," Mama began, clearly sorting her thoughts to make her point, "I read an article Dr. Drake published in the *Gazette*. It was about cholera and, most importantly, it was about the cure for cholera." She let that sink in. "Dr. Drake contends that if the disease is caught early enough, at first signs of bowel or stomach distress. . ." She paused delicately, perhaps a bit embarrassed by her subject, but she continued stoutly, "he says if you catch the disease early enough that it can be cured."

"How?" I asked, for this was the first time I'd heard of this. Up until this conversation, I had not even known it could be survived.

"Well, he said to take to your bed immediately, keep warm, drink hot tea, bring on perspiration, and send

71

word to your doctor. And he said the terror that cholera caused was as dangerous as the disease itself."

"I have the terrors of it," confessed Aunt Charlotte.

"But I know you'd agree we mustn't let ourselves be ruled by terror," Mama said. Aunt Charlotte shot Mama a begrudging look of agreement and we all sat quietly for a moment, thinking about what had been said.

Jackie began to babble. It looked for all the world he was talking to the wooden spoon he'd been using for ballast. He was holding it in his chubby little hand and talking to it, his tone changing from newsy to stern to excited. "I wish I knew what that was about," Mama said, and we all laughed, trying to imagine what he was so earnestly saying to that spoon. We spoke no more of cholera, but I have remembered many times what we said that day. For cholera did strike Lexington, and it started right there on Second Creek.

Chapter VIII

Cholera

It was the very first day of June, a beautiful morning when my world collapsed. King came running in, banging the door, coughing and hacking and gasping for air by the time he reached the servants' entrance to the house. "Cal!" he yelled. I was on the stairs, scrubbing as usual, and when I heard him I dropped my brush into the bucket and jumped up, immediately alarmed at the fear in his voice. "Cal, go quick. It's your Ma and the baby both," he called as I came clattering down the steps.

Without another word, not even pulling off my apron or putting on a bonnet, I ran as fast as I could down High and Upper toward home. My heart was pounding so loudly and the only thought I could form was the one word, *please*. That and *please, no*. As I turned onto Town Branch I saw Aunt Charlotte in her buggy. She was dressed in traveling clothes and pulled up when she saw me.

"Aunt Charlotte, what's happening?" I cried.

Tears ran down her cheeks. "I've got to go, Cal. God forgive me, there's nothing more I can do for them. Come with me and save yourself."

I stared at her for an endless second and ran on. When I burst into the house, the change from bright sunlight to almost total blackness rendered me momentarily blind, but the smell of human waste and sickness smacked me like a wall. I heard a moan and made my way to Mama's bed. She lay with Jackie in her arms, both of them covered in vomit and lying in their own filth. I slipped on the slimy, foul floor as I came near, but did not fall. She had been biting her hand to keep from crying out and there was blood on her from that too. She was writhing with cramp, the pain slicing through her most terribly. Jackie was asleep but no, truly, it was something deeper than that. I could barely see him breathing.

"Mama," I whispered, for shock and terror had taken my voice. I grabbed her bloody hands and leaned over her.

Tears ran down her ravaged face; she looked old, sunken, gray. "I'm so sorry, daughter."

"No, Mama, save your strength. I'm here, you're going to be fine, both of you, don't you worry, just rest," I babbled, without the slightest idea what to do.

I heated water and tried to clean them both a bit, but it wasn't long before Mama too fell into that state deeper than sleep from which both she and Jackie never awoke. When I saw they were both dead, I began to cry and could not stop. I cried so hard, so loudly;

deep horrible sobs wrenched up from the very center of myself. I choked on my tears until I vomited, and thought perhaps I was catching it too and I would die with them and perhaps that's what I wanted just then. At one point I stumbled out onto the porch for air and found King sitting there quietly as if he had been waiting for me. He wrapped me in a hug and pulled me onto his lap as he used to do when I was little. He rocked me like a baby.

"They're gone, King, they're gone. Both of them," I sobbed.

He patted me gently and soothed me as we used to do for Jackie if he fell into a fret. "Now, now. Now, now, young Cal." But in fact there was nothing more to say. Mama and Jackie were dead.

I felt dizzy and when I finally let go of King I stumbled around on the porch as if I were a drunk. Looking back, I realize that with Mama's death I had literally had the legs knocked out from under me. I would be finding my way without her and I had no idea how or even if it could be done.

King told me to go to the shed he'd built behind Aunt Charlotte's and fetch his cart. He assured me he would do what needed doing in the house and then we would get them to the burying ground. I followed his orders blindly and stumbled, lurching, still unsteady on my feet, to fulfill my errand. This was a simple cart he used to haul rocks for fence building. I wheeled it back to the house where he had laid out Mama and Jackie, wrapped in the filthy quilt they died in.

"It all has to get buried or burned so we might as well do it this way," King explained, as he gently lifted this bundle, my family, and arranged it in his cart. He picked up a shovel from our porch and together we walked out the creek path and into town. Little could we have known that before the month was out, Lexington would open up a new cemetery to hold the hundreds and hundreds of bodies stricken by cholera. Mama and Jackie were only some of the first to die.

I sat under an old oak tree that was only beginning to green as I listened to King dig. It took a long long time. I don't remember what I thought about during those hours, I have very little memory at all of that evening. But I do know that eventually we put them in the ground. There was no casket and no way to get one just then as I had no money, so the quilt served as their shroud and they were entombed in the earth.

King said the words while I stood still, tears I no longer felt, streaming down my face. "Lord," King intoned, "we are entrusting two of your finest souls back into your care. Please welcome them home and send comfort to those they leave behind." I felt numb and blank. I didn't even think I could walk back to the Hunt-Adams mansion but King stayed with me and saw me home. Mama and Jackie, my whole family, now dead and never coming back.

I do remember walking straight up the back stairs and into my room. Taking off only my boots, I climbed under the covers and lay down. I had no idea what time it was, nor did I care. I had only one thought: I could not go on alone. I slept and woke and slept again and woke and slept. How many days did I stay in my bed? I'm not sure. I do remember Mrs. Alice coming and going, and one morning as I lay staring at the wall, she offered me a cup of tea. My lips were parched and cracked and the hot sugary liquid burned going down, but somehow it woke me up. I could feel the warmth spreading through my body and it was that day I managed to get up, wash myself as best I could, brush out my tangled hair and go downstairs to the kitchen.

I was exhausted by the short trip down the stairs and sat dumbly in a chair unsure of what to do next or how. Mrs. Alice put a bowl of porridge in front of me and then spread molasses over it. Although I doubted I could eat it, I found I could. In fact, against my will, I was hungry. It seemed wrong and disrespectful but my body insisted on its rights, and slowly I finished the bowl and did feel strength returning. That day and for the many, many days that followed, Mrs. Alice and I lived quietly. She never spoke and I could think of nothing I wanted or needed to say.

Many evenings King came by and gave us the news. It was always bad. People were dying by the dozens, then scores, every day. At first, most of the dead were on Second Creek and up Town Branch, but quickly the horror spread throughout the town. Even doctors from Transylvania died, as did their wives and children, businessmen, council men, whole families were destroyed in a single day. We were helpless against the relentless onslaught of this raging evil. Just as we had read in the paper, people healthy in the morning were dead that night.

King worked steadily, fed mostly on whiskey and cigars, carting corpses to the cemetery and putting them into the ground. I could hear the wheels of his hand cart rattling on the cobblestone streets blocks away. A few constables and citizen volunteers worked as well, but as soon as one of their number caught sick, most of them disappeared. With so many strong men gone, they were far behind on burying. Most anyone who could, fled town. By the hundreds, families packed into carts and carriages, some even on foot; rushing as Aunt Charlotte had, they left the cursed city.

All day long fires burned as blankets, clothes, and even furniture of the dead were destroyed. A constant pall of gray smoke hovered over the city and the church bells tolled relentlessly throughout the day, counting the dead. At night, when I could not sleep—for my old companion, insomnia, was back—I would creep out to one of the balconies. From where the mansion sat, I could see for miles over town. The air smelled of loss, of ashes, of rotting corpses, for the bodies lay piled high along the roads. I could see rats scurrying about and packs of dogs roamed the streets. Always, day and night, the fires burned and the crying and the cursing would puncture the night like stab wounds. Sometimes a woman would scream shrilly and as loud as if she was being attacked.

These sounds of terror, fury, and despair echoed up from all around. The poor and the rich seemed almost equally cursed, although as is ever true, the poor suffered more. Sometimes a man, worked wild by grief and maybe whiskey, could be heard cursing God, shouting threats and then suddenly he too would be sobbing, pleading, sending up promises as useless as his threats. These were the sounds of a broken city. I would sit for hours on the back porch, listening, glimpsing the splendor of the stars beyond the smoky cloud of misery that engulfed us.

No one knew what caused the plague, so the terror of catching it lay everywhere. Was it in the air we breathed? Perhaps the water we drank? Did we catch it from each other? Was it really a curse from God? I didn't know the answers, but the uncertainty made for an atmosphere of suspicion and fear. And King? He handled the contaminated bodies all day and most of the night. Why didn't he get sick? Later, we would joke he was too pickled to catch anything, but at the time there was no humor, only fear. One night over tea (his liberally laced with Mr. Hunt-Adams's whiskey—yes, I did this, because I thought he needed it), I asked him, "King, aren't you afraid of catching it?"

He pondered a bit and chewed the cigar stub that was always in his mouth, then said, "Yes, honey, I reckon I am. From what I see, and you, God bless you have seen it too, it's a horrible way to go."

That took me back to the moment when I really took in the picture of Mama and Jackie lying dead in their soiled and stinking bed. I couldn't say anything, but I nodded to show I knew what he meant.

"I don't want to get it," he said. "That's for sure."

"But, King, aren't you scared of dying?" It shocked me that I spoke so plainly to him, but the words rushed out before I thought of them.

He smiled a wobbly smile and took a sip of his drink. "I reckon I am. I'm going to have a lot to answer for when I meet my Maker, but I'm more afraid of living with myself if I don't do what I know I should. Now there's a mouthful for you, Calendula," he said, laughing. "And much as I'd like to stay and jaw with you a little longer, I better get back at it." He got up to leave and I went to put my arms around him in a hug, but he wouldn't let me. "Can't have the sole surviving Farmer getting sick, now can we?" he said. "Let's just play it safe till this storm of dying is played out."

During the days, Mrs. Alice and I maintained some sort of routine. We ate very little, a piece of bread and maybe a smear of butter. We nibbled on whatever we found in the larder; created meals from odd concoctions of things: hardtack and canned beans and vegetables, jellies, salted meat.

Neither one of us could bear to venture outside. The one time I tried, I got down to Main Street and saw an old black-clad preacher man who stood in the square raging that this was punishment, that the dead were sinners. With every toll of the bell he pointed his arms to heaven. "Repent! Repent! Repent or die!" he screamed in a raspy, hate-filled voice. I turned and ran back to the mansion as fast as I could to get away from him. Otherwise I might have done him physical harm for implying that Mama and Jackie were responsible for their own deaths.

My blood boiled and for once I spoke to Mrs. Alice, angry tears accompanying my narrative. "He's so wrong," I said. "Mama and Jackie were not sinners. Neither was Dr. Mills or Annie Jefferson or Mildred Dudley or Morton Todd or ..." I broke down sobbing at the futility of trying to name all the dead. I cried as I had not done since I'd come back to the mansion. The bout of crying the day of their deaths had drained me, until then, of tears.

Mrs. Alice put a tentative hand on my shoulder and patted me lightly. I let the misery of my aloneness sweep over me, the injustice of that wretched man blaming the very ones who had suffered. I have never been able to care for religious people who use misfortune as an example to others, as if misfortune only visits itself on the sinners.

Mrs. Alice and I spent long hours, days, and weeks in the basement, boiling, bleaching, rinsing, wringing, drying, and ironing the sheets and other linens of the household. At night she would put a kettle on the stove and I would build a fire and we would drink tea and eat some of the biscuits we both knew were not meant for the likes of us. News had come that the family was on the road home when they heard of the plague and turned around. Perhaps neither of us caught it because we had boiled and bleached it away. Perhaps we'll never know the answers to what causes it. I did not like not knowing but sometimes that's all there is.

I found Mrs. Alice's silence entirely sympathetic and comforting. King also never asked anything of me, never wanted to know how I was doing being an orphan. Their tact and kindness were lessons to me. Sometimes, the bereaved person wants nothing more than to be left alone; at least that is how it was for me.

Chapter IX

Rosalie

As had happened all year, just as I was falling into a habit, a pattern, a feeling of familiarity, a regularity about the days, everything changed again. This time it happened in the middle of the night sometime at the end of June. (Time was hard to catch hold of, as isolated as we were.) I awoke with a jolt to a scream that sounded raw and unmistakably frightened. For a moment I lay still, listening, but when the scream became words, "Help me, Jesus, help me," Mrs. Alice and I looked straight at each other through the moonlight and both of us jumped out of bed.

We ran, barefoot and hair flying, down the steps, for the sound was close, somewhere very near and the need was clearly urgent. A teenage girl was in Appleman's Alley that runs behind the Hunt-Adams property. Her name was Rosalie and she was a slave girl of the Abercrombie family, a girl maybe three or four years older than me, who I knew casually from around town. What was killing her was not the plague, it was a little girl, her little girl, who slipped out of her mother's body just as her mother was slipping into the arms of death. The transition happened within minutes.

We arrived, Mrs. Alice and I, just as the baby's head was crowning. I had been with Aunt Charlotte when she and Mama brought Jackie into the world so I knew a little of the magic. But this, this was so different. Poor Rosalie had gotten as far as the alley before the pains became too much for her to continue and she dropped in a heap. Her feet were bleeding but it was hard to even know that because of all the blood gushing out of her. It was as though some secret artery had broken loose for the blood literally pumped out. There was no way to stop it. What we did was save the baby girl.

I tried to tend to Rosalie, pillowing her head on my lap and crooning to her as one does. Useless silly words in a desperate moment, but it was all I had to give her. She was almost gone by the time we got there, exhaustion and blood loss were taking her to the other shore; the same shore that claimed Mama and my baby brother. She was still conscious or maybe still somewhat conscious in those few minutes and I assured her that her baby was going to be safe.

And suddenly, as if a candle had been lit inside my mind, I knew why Rosalie was running: she didn't want this baby born a slave. Unfortunately, she'd left too late and only got as far as this back alley. I told her, not knowing a thing about what I was saying, "We'll get her out of here, Rosalie, we'll get her free." She must have known I was only a young white girl who knew very little of the ways of the world, but her face softened and she died a little quieter. I tell myself that story anyway.

I began to feel I was cursed, that it was my fortune to sit with people as they died. Having done so now with three people in as many weeks was taking a toll on "the balance of your mind" as Mama used to call it. Self-pity is a tar pit and I knew it, but I could feel myself slogging my way over to it. Meanwhile, Mrs. Alice bit the cord and tied the baby off, a motherless child from her very first breath. And a full-throated little thing. She had wonderful lungs and a lusty appetite for life. We (I) named her Rose, mostly after her mother, but secretly a little bit after me. We were both named for flowers, a distinction only a Lily, a Violet, or a Daisy can appreciate. It was little enough to give her, but I wanted us to have a connection.

Mrs. Alice signaled for me to get sheets and toweling from the house. We wrapped Rosalie's sad and bloodied body gently and between the two of us, we carried her in from the alley to a table on the porch outside the kitchen. I would go for King at daybreak and he could add her to the mounds of dead accumulating at the cemetery gates. Rose we rubbed down and wrapped up in clean white cotton. She had a full head of black curly hair and a cheery, almost bossy way about her from the very beginning. I realized she need never know the story of her birth. Why weigh her down with so much sadness right at the start? I would keep it to myself, as Mrs. Alice did everything.

Mrs. Alice mimed writing to me, and although

I wasn't sure, I ran up to our room to retrieve my notebook and pencil. With a steady slow hand, she printed one word: goat. I was astonished. Because she doesn't speak, most people, and this included me, often presumed she was deaf as well. But had I ever wondered, I knew now she listened to everything. She must have heard me describing Aunt Charlotte's goat, Nanny, to Cook or maybe Jimmy in the laundry. Whatever the case, she was one step ahead of me in thinking about the baby. I nodded and slipped out before dawn to go round up Nanny if I could.

Fortunately, Nanny was placidly nibbling on a fence post on the now-deserted cornfield of one of our neighbors. She came with me quietly and I was most grateful. Even better, luck had it that I saw King on my way back and told him what happened and how now we had a baby and a corpse, and he had to come take care of the one and we would take care of the other.

Mrs. Alice, it seemed, possessed all kinds of useful knowledge about babies and goats. She made teas for Nanny to drink and pulled and rubbed on Nanny's teats till she started up with milk again. And by then it was a good thing too, for Rose was crying mad with hunger. Mrs. Alice also knew how to wrap Rose so snug she would calm. It was just like a papoose I had seen one day in town, tied onto a flat board. The whole Indian family was passing through town and I remember wondering which of us got the biggest eyeful that day. We were so foreign to each other.

The thing about Rose was she was so full of herself,

so her own person. She was also so interested, right from the beginning, in what was going on around her. Maybe most babies are like this, I wouldn't know, but with Jackie, he mostly just slept the first month or so after he was born. Not little Rose, no, she slept in three six-hour stretches, and was awake and aware the rest of the time. She was always waving her little hand, so perfectly made, her little fingernails so tiny and sweet. And babbling, Rose was another talker. In fact it is not too much to say she came out talking and hardly ever stopped. After she got finished crying over being born, she began to mumble, grumble, blow little spit bubbles and make baby noises.

I loved Rose as much as I have ever loved anyone. It was as though Mrs. Alice and I became her mothers together. We waited on her hand and foot and were pleased to do it. Nanny was well fed and gave good milk. We made thin gruels of boiled and smashed rice or maybe hominy. It was an odd thing to be cooking and caring. It felt prickly coming back to life, like a foot that has gone to "sleep." As the blood rushes in, the sensation is almost painful. For that is what happened; Rose brought me back to life, to love, her neediness pierced my numbness. Her gurgling engagement with the world and sighs of utter contentment bewitched me and warmed me and brought me out of my well of infinite sadness. Rose brought life, at least to me. She brought death to her mother, but I hope she never had to know that.

Chapter X

Rose

Fourth of July that year did not bring the President to Lexington. All the civic excitement and planning came to nothing. There was black mourning crepe hung in town, not bunting. Andrew Jackson stayed far away, as did everyone who could. Dozens of people were still dying daily. I softly sang the song I had practiced so long to baby Rose who seemed to like it very much. Mrs. Alice and I spent that day, and the ones after, passing this little bundle of joy between us and darting small shy smiles at each other as we again took up the duties of the living.

King was as besotted with Rose as Mrs. Alice and me. He had taken her mother to the burying ground and would see her into her grave in due time, but anytime he could, anytime he rested, he came to see "his baby." That's what he called her, "My baby." I guess we all felt protective of Rose; she was a well loved and well cared for infant. Who would have thought that in the midst of the worst epidemic Lexington had ever faced, in its darkest hour, there shone a little light up in the mansion on the hill. That light was Rose.

King, of course, would never hold her. For all we knew, the cholera was in his jacket. He handled hundreds of corpses and never caught it, whereas someone like Mama—she was such a clean woman—oh, never mind. I still struggle with my grief. Time doesn't seem to heal all wounds.

We had Rose from her birth at the end of June, to her departure at the beginning of August. For those six weeks, I was alive. I was up at all hours of the night, I was changing her little napkins and washing and rinsing and sometimes we would use rain water because it was extra soft. We were coaxing milk into her tummy and fed her with a sucking rag like we would have done for a pig or a pup. One day I heard music and realized I had been singing. It was a strange out of place sound but it had come out of me before I knew it. The song was a lullaby Mama used to sing and remembering her made me cry. That's the hard part about being alive, it hurts.

The cholera plague began to burn itself out by the middle of July and slowly, cautiously, a few citizens returned. One of the first to flee, Aunt Charlotte was one of the first to return. We'd heard, through King, a rumor that she'd died, but she was happy enough to prove that wrong. What she wasn't happy about was Rose. "We gotta get this baby out of here, Calendula. Now." I was holding Rose and instinctively clutched her closer to me. "What do you think gonna happen when your master and madam get back? Huh? Have you thought about that?"

Of course I had, a little. I avoided the thought mostly because I couldn't make anything work out the way I wanted it to. Not even in my imagination. Aunt Charlotte said what I knew to be true but denied out of despair. "That little baby belongs to the Abercrombies. She's their property, Calendula, and so is her mother. They ain't gonna be able to get Rosalie back, she's beyond their grip now, and I thank Jesus for that, but they sure ain't gonna just sit by and let you raise this child. Who you think her father is?"

That startled me. For some reason, exhaustion maybe, I hadn't thought that Rose must have a father. Would he want her? Why was Rosalie running when she died? Aunt Charlotte saw my confusion and made a sound of disgust. "Honey, look at that child, she's half white. Can't you see that?"

Now that she mentioned it, I could see, especially in contrast to the dark ebony of Aunt Charlotte's skin, that Rose was more brown than black and not a dark brown at that. So, what did that mean? I was thirteen and a half and still slow at understanding her meaning. Aunt Charlotte waited.

"Who?" I asked in desperation.

She shook her head sadly at me until I understood. "The master?" I asked in a small voice. She nodded and reached over to hug me when I started to cry. We squeezed Rose between us as we rocked back and forth. "What's going to happen?" I asked at last.

91

"That ain't for you to worry about," she said. "Let Aunt Charlotte work it out."

I hated that kind of an answer from an adult but at that point, I felt too rolled over by sadness to care.

I was not completely naïve about the true nature of many masters' relationships with their female slaves. Everyone knew, or so I heard at school, that men had appetites their wives couldn't satisfy (although what this actually meant worried me some). Anyway, what everyone knew was that white masters used their female slaves, sometimes just one, sometimes several, in a way they wouldn't use their wives. But either way, it made for babies. And I knew too that Rose, this precious bit of humanity that had been handed to me to hold and care for, was not mine. I was seen as a child myself at thirteen and it is only because I was such a wishful one I had not allowed myself to really think about what would happen to Rose.

It was about a week later that Rose disappeared. Aunt Charlotte said she had found a good family, traveling north, who took Rose with them. As all the slaves knew, what they had to do, once in Kentucky, was get across the Ohio. In the state of Ohio they could be free. But it was a perilous journey and I worried constantly that maybe they'd been caught and Rose was now a slave.

At that time, back in 1833, no one used the term Underground Railroad. All that came later, the naming of it, but slaves had been running away and white people and free blacks had been helping them since the very start of this abominable institution. As I said, I didn't know any other Freethinkers besides my mother but there were several Abolitionists in Lexington that Mama had admired. The Kentucky Abolitionist Society was formed so there must have been a tide of feeling all this time. I learned later where some of the safe places were in Lexington. It was dangerous work being a friend and all involved tried not to know more than needed.

So Rose disappeared and I tried to count her as alive, not dead, but found that missing her was much the same. Sometimes I actually writhed with pain when I gave in to missing her. I knew Aunt Charlotte had done the right thing. It was a chance for Rose to grow up free. I also knew that if the Abercrombies discovered Rose existed, they could and would claim her.

Rose filled a sad place in me, a place that longed to mother now that I was motherless, that wanted to save her as I couldn't save my own family. And on balance of it, Mrs. Alice and I did save her, but we couldn't keep her. The real truth is Rose was saving me. Before we had her, I woke and worked and ate and slept as one going through the motions only. But when Rose came, I began to live again. There was reason and even urgency to attend to affairs other than my own miseries. Rose saved me from the deadness that had entered me as a long chill. Now that she was gone, it was hard to manage and I didn't do very well.

Chapter XI

Sad and Mad

By the time the Hunt-Adamses did come back to town it was late August, and I had lain abed, neither awake nor asleep, for almost two weeks. All my life, at least since the events of this mighty year, I have had to guard myself against a strong tendency towards sloth. If idle, I can easily be overcome with melancholy and want to lie down. Thus, I have learned to keep myself occupied with meaningful or at least productive work. Mama used to warn me that idle hands were the devil's workshop and I have found for myself how true this is. A great sucking sadness stands ready to pull me under should I allow myself to brood. So I don't. I have forbidden brooding. I once met a Catholic nun who told me to count my blessings, not my troubles, and I have found this to be tolerably helpful advice.

That summer, the cholera summer, was surely the hardest I have ever endured. Rose was a little gift of light and life and laughter, but we had her for only a short time. Without Rose, I could not think of a reason to get up. I wasn't hungry and I wanted to see no one. All the linens in the entire mansion had already been washed and bleached and ironed and I had no intention of helping Mrs. Alice go through them again. She, however, seemed to find solace in the very work itself and did not mind that she was washing pristine cloth.

However, as all who have suffered as I did know, life goes on with or without your permission. Unwillingly, I was dragged back into the flow of the household as they descended on us with their noise and need. The grandmother had died while in Virginia and not of the cholera but simply old age. Other than that, however, they were all back and the house resumed its usual bustling pace. I dragged my feet and sullenly did all that was requested of me but no more. After perhaps a week of this, Cook sat me down to talk to me, as she said, "like a Dutch uncle."

"You are only hurting yourself with this mournful manner, Cal," Cook said. "I know you've been through a rough time, but you've got to look forward not back. Don't let the tragedies you've lived through permanently sour you. Do you understand me?"

Actually I did, but I merely shrugged an answer that could have been yes or no and went back to my chores. Cook had never seen Rose, and Aunt Charlotte had warned us strictly never to speak of her to anyone. I was certainly not alone that late summer in my sadness. The entire city remained in mourning. No colors were worn, only black and gray. There was no gaiety, no dancing, no music or theater, no parties.

Everyone had lost someone and many, like myself, had lost all.

The grand ladies of the town—and Mrs. Hunt-Adams could certainly be counted as one—were full of plans to provide for the orphans of the city. There were hundreds of us, maybe even more. Because of all the death and because of people running from it, the town had grown ragged and run-down. Yards were unkempt and overgrown, goats and cows and pigs and chickens were untended and ran loose, nibbling here and there as they chose. Most of the crops in the fields had been abandoned, and there was concern about having food enough to make it through winter.

King became a hero. He went from being the town laughingstock to a man who stood his ground and did his job when almost no one else would. The town council held a prayer day of Thanksgiving when the bells tolled all day, counting out the number of our dead. King was snoozing quietly in the back row of the courthouse, taking in the ceremonies, when he heard his name called and startled awake. "Cal, tell you the truth I thought for a minute it was God Almighty," he said, "telling me it was time to go. I practically forgot who William Solomon was. It was right nervous making, I tell you." He was saluted and called to the front to receive a medal of honor. Poor King. He was less used to admiration than to approbation and seemed stunned and puzzled by the attention. Aunt Charlotte had elbowed him awake when his name was called, and she told me he practically stumbled up the aisle. Those city men who knew him best thanked him (out of sight of Aunt Charlotte, under whose authority he was still indentured) with the currency he most valued—whiskey and cigars. But in court, he merely received the medal (which he showed me with shy pride) and a letter of commendation, which I read to him any time he wanted to hear it.

It was during this period, mostly in September, when I began to contemplate the inconceivable. Perhaps, I thought one day, there is no God. Perhaps we have made it all up out of a terrible yearning for life and death to make sense, to have meaning. This terrible thought came to me after sitting through one sermon too many about the just retribution of the Lord and our sinful ways. I could stand it no longer; Mama was no sinner and neither was Jackie. I grew furious at the implication that they were in some way responsible for their own deaths. Because I was never allowed to express an opinion as a child, and a girl child at that, I became inwardly rebellious. During prayer time, I would mutinously recite the alphabet or the times tables in my head rather than beseech the Almighty for any favor. In my thirteen-year-old way I was furious with God and especially furious with the people on earth who thought they knew what God wanted and why He did what He did.

Certainty has always seemed a refuge for the weak. There are too many mysteries in this world for the answers to be so simple. I became an unhappy Freethinker during this time, for I had exiled myself from the solace of a merciful God as well as the wrath of an angry one. I kept myself to myself and did not try to engage anyone in conversation. In retrospect, I was an unhappy, ungracious, and unpleasant girl to be around but I could find no way to alter my mood. Meanwhile the grand ladies of Lexington resolved to build an orphanage to house and school those, like me, who had no one. Many of the meetings held for this project were in the Hunt-Adams mansion. Endless cups of tea and dainty cakes were consumed as the women planned.

The power of the ladies has too often been underestimated. It was clear in this case that the ladies were the ones who decided on the right action, and it was the ladies who then went home to their husbands and raised the money their project required. And sure enough, a new building was speedily erected. One businessman in town had donated some five or six acres for the orphanage, just up past Third Street where it intersected with Broadway. In the fall of 1833, the plot was on the very outskirts of town, but this soon changed as the town grew up to and around the orphanage and even beyond. The orphanage would hold one hundred children. I should clarify that it would only serve white children. Although there were at least as many black orphans as white ones, the ladies thought only of the whites. The slave orphans would be cared for by their master and as for any free black orphans, it seemed they would have to shift for themselves. The ladies were quite proud of themselves for establishing the

Lexington Orphan Asylum. From the back stairs I overheard many self-congratulatory parties where the tinkling laughter, the light froth of conversation, and the clinking of china and silver resounded throughout the house.

The reader may conclude that I was embittered and angry and indeed, unfortunate as it is to admit to, you would be quite correct. In truth this anger made me feel further away from Mama than ever. She was such a gentle person, so fair and kind, she would hardly have recognized this closed-down daughter who muttered at her chores and frowned at everyone. Mama was brave in that she could speak out when she thought something was wrong, but she was not bitter. Even after all the disappointment Pa caused all of us, I never heard her utter an angry word about him.

Mama despised slavery and all its manifestations, just as she also disapproved of the power that wealth had in our young nation, but somehow her feelings, as intense as they were, made her a better person. She was not paralyzed with rage at the unfairness of the world. She burned with fervor, and as her daughter, I knew how passionate she could be, but it was a fire that gave her energy, purpose, even humor. I, on the other hand, could barely put together a civil sentence to anyone during this time. My rage and emptiness made me only tired and irritable, disagreeable, and at least in my mind, since not even I dared to express such feelings, I grew sarcastic.

Sarcasm is an interesting word in that the root of it

means to bite and tear the flesh, which is exactly what my bitter thoughts were meant to do. Oddly, there was no pleasure in this, merely a twisted sort of satisfaction that I had, at least to myself, proved the other person to be a fool. It was a lonely time in my life and I was making it lonelier by making it hard for anyone to come near me.

I was surrounded by well-meaning people and that infuriated me all the more. I could scorn easier than I could mourn and that is what I did. I might have become permanently warped in this sour and bitter way if not for King. He and Mrs. Alice and I had survived the summer together. We shared the horrors, the smells and sights of the corpses piling, we shared the fear and the isolation, and King and I shared the loss of Mama and Jackie. Not in the same way, but it was a bond.

King was always kind to me so it was no different for him to be gentle with me now, he'd gentled me all my life with his smiles and his simple jests and his boozy, rumpled sweetness. He didn't try to cheer me up, unlike Cook, and I found his casual usual manner with me a huge relief. He was about the only person I could halfway stand to be with, and now that the family was back, our kitchen nights were no longer ours, and I almost never saw him. Needless to say, this made me mad.

But one day, because I had my half day, I spent a few pennies in the market on some of Mrs. Simpson's honey. Hers is known to be the sweetest and October is the best time to buy it. This bit of honey was a small peace offering to Aunt Charlotte for I had been truly rude when we last saw each other, and she had let me know how unhappy she was with my attitude. Unfair as I knew it to be, I was still angry at her for making Rose disappear. Nonetheless, Aunt Charlotte and King were as close to relatives, to family, as I had in this world and I was fearful of Aunt Charlotte leaving me again as she did when the cholera started. I knew that wasn't completely fair either; she didn't leave me, personally, she was running panicked for her life, but thinking, logic, and reasoning have their limits. Some-times—and, sadly, for me this was one occasion—no matter how logically I explained to myself that she had a perfect right to leave, and was probably even right to leave, I held it against her anyway. She left Mama, and though I tried not to, I carried the weight of a grudge against her.

So that day's honey was supposed to be a small step toward mending the rift. If I couldn't mend it in my heart, I could at least mend it by my actions. Mama used to counsel, "If you can't feel your way into the right action, act your way into the right feeling." Basi-cally she was saying if I know something is the right thing to do, but I don't want to do the right thing, I should do it anyway and pretend I enjoyed it.

This particular advice was given when I was being bothered by an overly talkative younger girl at Dame School. This Mary Wallis tagged along and wanted my company far more than I wanted hers. She monopolized my recesses with useless chatter, and asked me the most ignorant questions about passages we were studying. Sometimes she went out of her way to walk with me down to Town Branch. I tried to be polite, but she was annoying. After complaining about this girl to Mama, who by the way was entirely unsympathetic, I admitted that yes, possibly, very possibly Mary was lonely and trying to make a friend; and, yes, perhaps she just didn't know how to do it. "Maybe she's never had a friend," said Mama. "So how would she know how to be one? You, daughter, are the lucky one here. You have had friends, have friends now. It's your place to show her how to do it. So you don't feel it in your heart, do it like you did and see what happens."

So following her advice, I more or less pretended to be nice to Mary. And strangely, it worked. The more I pretended to like her and take time for her with a smile on my face, the more I actually came to enjoy her company, at least somewhat. She never became my "cup of tea" as the saying goes, but by pretending to like her I made our relations much friendlier and it actually benefited us both at school for we practiced elocution with each other and sometimes played duets on Mrs. Rutledge's pianoforte.

So I was trying to act my way back into Aunt Charlotte's good graces. As usual for me, the walk from the Hill down to Second Creek lifted my spirits, and that afternoon the trees in the distance were looking like a quilt pieced with beautifully harmonious colors.

I shifted my eyes toward the creek when I walked by Mama's house. I knew King was sleeping there, but except for the morning after Rose was born, when I ran to find Nanny, I had not been back and or been inside. When I got to Aunt Charlotte's house, I found her and King both sitting at the table. Aunt Charlotte was working with some leaves and roots, doubtless in preparation for one of her medicines, and King was mending the harness she used for Abel, her horse. They both greeted me and invited me to join them at the bench, which I did.

When I gave the honeycomb to Aunt Charlotte, she said pertly, instead of thanking me, "Seems to me you be the one need sweetening up." I looked down, not meeting her eyes and secretly thought she was right but it made me sullen and my misery deepened.

King looked up and said, "Honey? Why I'd love a bite of honey and a biscuit. We got any of those biscuits left over? We got anything to drink? I'm working up a powerful thirst and I hadn't even got to the hard part yet," he said, shaking the leather in his hands and giving me a wink.

Aunt Charlotte shot him a disapproving glance but actually went to the stove, stirred the embers and set her big black cast iron tea kettle to boil. She warmed up the morning's biscuits and served them with a dab of butter and the honey; it was a warming sweet treat.

"Sweet girl," King said as we finished, "be a lamb and run yonder to your house and get my baccy sack."

And without a thought I did as he said. As soon

as I opened the door and saw our house, I went into a swoon of some sort. I didn't fall down, but I lost a deal of time just looking around, thinking to this day I know not what. Perhaps just reeling in the emptiness of the place. At some point, after the sun had moved in the sky, I stiffly walked back to Aunt Charlotte's. As I came in the door, she said crossly, "Where on earth have you been, girl? Look at you, white as a sheet, like you've seen a ghost or…" She clapped her hand over her mouth and went to grab me but I dodged her and don't know where I might have gone had King not taken me onto his lap and rocked me like a big old bear rocking its cub. Suddenly I was about ten years old and feeling how much I missed Mama. This time no sarcastic wit could protect me, this time I felt it and it hurt. I cried and cried until I could cry no more and for some reason after that, I wasn't quite as angry as I had been. King rocked me and crooned to me like the hurt pup I was, and I took in the sounds of his gravelly tones without having to understand anything else.

Chapter XII

A Choice

Weekly visits to Aunt Charlotte and King sustained me throughout the autumn. I didn't go back into our family's house again during that time because memories overwhelmed me. Aunt Charlotte tended to me furiously with her potions. My monthly courses had stopped in the summer, due, she said, to strain and worry and near starvation. I hadn't realized it but during June and July I lost a lot of weight. The misery of June and the busyness of July, caring for Rose, had left me downright skinny, tired, and pale. Aunt Charlotte fed me broths of beef neck bones and greens, all manner of herbs, most of which were hard to swallow for being so awful tasting.

That fall was a somber one; it seemed even the little children did not laugh as they used to. There was no play or frivolity anywhere. Although I had softened some from the crust of anger that had surrounded me, I too felt low a good deal of the time, but, then again, so did everyone.

The ladies met at least twice a week, drank gallons of tea, coffee, and sherry, ate hundreds of Cook's pastries, dirtied all the best china—which was quite a trial to wash and dry and not break "or you'll see what happens," Cook threatened—and somehow they planned and saw to the actual construction on the Orphan Asylum.

The Orphan Asylum rose quickly, a sturdy limestone building with three floors. The top was for the boys dormitory, the middle for the girls, and the first floor was for meals, lessons, church, and whatever other activities they planned. The building was designed to hold one hundred children, fifty boys and fifty girls. There would be a matron to manage the children, several slaves who had been "donated" to do the heavy work, and the ladies themselves proposed to form a rotation and visit on a regular basis to supervise the orphans' lives. A teacher would be hired in January and school would commence.

On the property was a large run-down apple orchard, and beyond that a hemp field, a barn with room for three cows to provide milk; plus chickens, a goat, and a large garden plot in which the orphans were expected to grow their own victuals come spring and summer. It was an ambitious plan, and as it began to take shape, I wavered between curiosity about living there to abject misery at the thought of losing the independence and income I had gained as a working girl.

"Law," King said, "just think of all those children in one place. Now that could be a sight."

"It's a big place," Aunt Charlotte responded thoughtfully. "Abel and I were out there just the other day to see how it's coming. I heard Widow McKeever agreed to be Matron." She shot a look at me and we both grinned. Widow McKeever could handle a hundred orphaned children if anyone could. She was well known to the town children for the immaculate way she kept her "lawn." If you were foolish enough to cut across her lot, she would be out of the house and on you before you took your next breath. Her brisk no-nonsense ways were legend in Lexington and she seemed (and proved to be) an excellent choice.

A silence fell as we thought about a home with one hundred children. Then King turned to me and said gently, "What about you, little one?"

Him calling me "little one" made hot tears spring to life, burning the back of my throat, and I had to concentrate to control myself. I stared at the table. Tactfully, Aunt Charlotte brought me a bowl of potatoes and a knife so I began to peel. It was good to have something to do, even fumble-fingered as I am. Only King would be sweet enough to wonder about me and naïve enough to think I had a choice. But as of the day before, miraculously, I did.

"I heard they offered for you to stay there on the Hill with them, ain't that right?" Aunt Charlotte asked.

I nodded and answered, "Yes, that's part of why I'm here." In fact, just the day before, Mrs. Hunt-Adams had summoned me into her morning room. Cook made me put on a clean apron, adjust my cap, and wash

109

my face and hands before I could respond. Hesitantly, I traversed the immense gleaming distance between the kitchen door and the morning room. The very air on the other side of the door is different, somehow rarer and richer. Mrs. Hunt-Adams sat at her desk, a large, ornately carved mass of cherry wood with wonderful little places for all a writer might need. I had admired this very desk often during my time dusting in this room back in the days before. That is how we all spoke of it in those days. Before. Before the cholera killed off hundreds of us, before we ran or stayed, it made no matter, the echoes of our loved ones' dying groans and moans will echo in our ears forever. Before we learned what it is to be afraid for our lives. Now is after.

"Ma'am?" I inquired, dipping a smart curtsy.

Mrs. Hunt-Adams looked up and the sun from the garden window behind her spilled on her hair, highlighting the golds and yellows and auburns. She was one of the loveliest women I had ever seen and even now, I must stand by that. She had a serenity that seemed to shimmer around her. Maybe it was the perfume. I had never smelled it on the women I knew, like Mama or Mrs. Rutledge or Aunt Charlotte (although she sometimes smells of vanilla). Mrs. Hunt-Adams not only smelled of something secret and silky, the air around her smelled that way too. She brought with her wherever she went a scent of that something that identified her.

"Oh, yes. Calendula," she said as she bade me come to her. In her mouth my name sounded like honey.

She turned away from her desk and gestured that I should take a seat, which I did, carefully choosing a small hardback chair with an embroidered cushion. I composed myself and waited. She gazed at me a moment, a soft unfocused blue gaze that nevertheless seemed to see me clearly. She cleared her throat and said in her deep slow burnt amber voice, "I am terribly sorry for your loss. I heard that both your dear mother and baby brother were victims of this awful plague." She paused.

I thanked her politely, swallowed back memories and waited. It seemed strange to me she had waited months to tell me this.

"Have you given any thought to your future, Calendula, now that," she looked uncomfortable but finished, "you are an orphan."

"Yes, ma'am," I answered truthfully. I had been carefully considering this very point. Clearly, Mama would want me to pursue my education and the Orphan Asylum seemed the best way to do that. The school they were to open in January would be for both boys and girls, something I had never experienced at Dame Rutledge's School for Young Ladies. I was curious as to what the classroom would be like. "I'm thinking to go to the orphanage," I said, "when they open in December and start my schooling in January." She waited. I waited. "My mama would have wanted me to get my education. Mama was uncommonly in favor of learning." I started to add "especially for girls," which was true, but something stopped me.

111

Mrs. Hunt-Adams shifted prettily on her seat and rearranged the flawless folds of her gown. "Yes, your mother was quite an advocate of education. Free, public education if I remember rightly." She somehow made it sound like a disease. "However, now that you are on your own," and here she leveled her blue gaze on me, "you need to consider your future. What use, after all, is an education to a girl like you; I mean, really?"

I opened my mouth to reply but saw the question had been rhetorical. A girl like me? What kind of girl did she think I was? What she meant, of course, was what would a tweeny do with an education. And she had a point. But I had been raised by an uncommon woman. Mama said my education was my fortune and my own responsibility. I should never ever quit studying and learning, no matter my circumstances there would always be something to be learned. And learning was precious beyond knowing. Not everyone enjoys learning for the thrill of getting a new thought. But I, the Freethinker's daughter, do.

Mrs. Hunt-Adams, however, was completely unhampered by the notion that a working girl, her tweeny, might actually want to go to school. Had I been one of the quality, she would have seen to it I learned piano, dancing, embroidery, and all the other skills I would need in that world. But in the world of the back stairs, which is where I existed for her, there was no need at all to clutter up a mind with history, science, or literature. She had plucked me like a drowned puppy out of the human flotsam that had washed up literally on her doorstep, the night of the flood. She rarely thought of me and almost never saw me. But now she made me an offer: she would keep me on with the possibility of promotion to house maid. Cook's report on my progress under her had been satisfactory and Mrs. Hunt-Adams would like to keep me, "as a charity." Further, if I so wished, she would afford me two hours a week for study instead of the one my mother bargained for. "However," she concluded coldly, "if you still wish to go to the Orphan Asylum, I will not stop you."

I was flustered, completely flummoxed, and I remember sitting there with my mouth open before I attended to it. Suddenly, I had a choice. Completely unsure of what to do, for once in my life I did the right thing. I stalled. "Madam, may I have a measure of time to consider your offer before giving you my answer? As to my future?" My tone was humble and to my intense irritation I could not stop the shaking in my voice.

She looked surprised. Her eyebrows rose delicately in a moue of astonishment. "What? Do you not wish to be able to save up enough money to launch yourself into the world in a few more years? A girl with no family, no wedding portion? Well, it's nothing to me, Calendula." She shook her head and brushed her silk skirt to show how truly nothing it was (I was) to her. "But I must insist on two weeks' notice if you intend to leave. We shall be obliged to find and train another girl, but naturally, do as you wish. Young people always do these days. Good day."

It was already November and I would move, if that was what I chose, in only a few weeks. November was upon us in an agony of thanksgiving. All of Lexington went to church several times a week to make fervent and long prayers of repentance and remembrance. It was as though the souls of the five hundred dead in the summer still floated in the dark gray looming clouds that covered our town that autumn. If I were to move to the orphanage in December when it opened, I needed to give my notice now. But the idea of saving my own money was diverting and riveting in the extreme.

I was not surprised that Aunt Charlotte knew of my offer. She had the uncanny ability to keep her ear to the ground and know what was what with nearly everyone in town, black and white. As I laid out my dilemma to her, she rocked in her chair and just listened.

"So I have to make up my mind now," I concluded. "What do you think I should do?"

"I don't know, child. I just don't know how to advise you. What are you thinking on it?"

"Well, I see the benefit of staying on," I said. "I could save enough money in two or more years, if I don't spend it and save, to buy..." I stopped there and she waited. "Well, I don't know, but you see what I mean. On the one hand, I'd be, well, not rich, but I'd have something. I might be able to save one hundred dollars, Aunt Charlotte. That's a lot of money."

"Hmm. No doubt about that," she agreed in that dangerously neutral voice I had long ago learned to beware of from both her and Mama.

114

"So," I concluded as humbly as I could, "I'm taking advice on what to do."

Aunt Charlotte smiled at me. "Honey, I really don't know what to tell you. Seems like you laid out the reasons on both sides of it. You know what your mama would say about now."

I knew what Mama would have told me: "You need to consult your inner wisdom." This was a concept I'd grown up with. Mama said we all knew the right thing to do deep inside ourselves; the hard part was getting quiet enough to hear the inner voice.

Many times as a child I had been told to consult my inner wisdom about the decisions I faced. Like the time I stole a penny candy from the store and Mama found out. I had to decide whether to tell Mr. Rosen what I'd done and make restitution, or have her tell him. That was an awful dilemma for a six-year-old with a sweet tooth, but I did consult my inner wisdom and go back and apologize and repay him the penny, which I then had to work to repay to Mama. I went because my inner wisdom told me it would be awful, but it would be better if I owned up to my crime. And it was.

For most of that year, all my life's decisions had been made for me, first by the flood, then by the cholera, then by Aunt Charlotte taking Rose. But now the next step on my path was really up to me and I was torn. I had tried to be quiet and let the answer arise, but I couldn't seem to do it. I do think Mama would have chosen the orphanage for me, but of course had she lived I wouldn't be an orphan.

I wasn't eager to give up the independence I had gained, living in the mansion, earning a wage. As hard as the work was, once I adjusted to it, I found it was merely drudgery, not torture. And drudgery can be managed in large part by a lively imagination. Daydreamers are given a bad name and deserve it if all they do is daydream, but if one can separate the hands (deep in soap and suds) from the head (high in the clouds) you can have any manner of wonderful adventures while the back stairs get scrubbed, the row gets hoed, or the sheets get ironed.

I had simply assumed the next step for me would be the Orphan Asylum, mostly because I knew that was what Mama would want. She valued learning like other people value money. When I learned to read, to actually make the letters jump into words, she had a party and invited all our friends from up and down the creek and even made me a cake.

"You're free now, daughter," Mama toasted me. "You have the keys to the kingdom. Enter and enjoy forever!" Everyone (about half of whom couldn't read themselves) clapped and whistled and made toasts to me and to reading and to Freethinking and to the cake. I must have been six or seven and I remember the party and reading a page of *Poor Richard's Almanac* and being the center of so much attention. I loved all that in a shy somewhat overwhelmed way. I remember the weight I felt, the heaviness of the responsibility no one talked about. If I could read, ignorance was really no longer an option.

Now that I had a choice I was mortally tempted and completely unsure of how to proceed. November 30th was rapidly approaching and I knew my decision was due. I was most certainly not looking forward to the change from being my own person—after all there was only one tweeny at the Hunt-Adams's—to being one of a hundred children who would be made to line up; to live in crowded, if not overcrowded, rooms; to eat and do every thing as one among many. Now that the choice of staying had been offered, it looked very tempting to me. I referred earlier to the lethargy that attends melancholia and certainly the urge to stay as I was, if only for another year or two, seemed preferable to another upheaval. I was deeply tired of change. But then there was Mama to consider. I was torn.

In the end, it was a dream that helped me. I fell asleep the night before the last day, after hours of fretful and fruitless thoughts and many more unsatisfactory attempts toward hearing my inner wisdom. I felt like a complete failure, worse, that I was failing my mother who had taught me to do this. Now, when I really needed to know what to do, I was lost. And that night, I dreamed of my mother. She was holding me on her lap and rocking in her old chair by the fire. She was stroking my hair and whispering in my ear that she would always love me, not to worry. Humming and calming me with her love. Somehow I was curled on her lap but not hurting her, she held me easily as if I was little. She murmured love words into my hair and told me again and again she would always love me. I awoke drenched in tears I hadn't realized I cried. Waking seemed a horrible punishment, to be pushed out, unwillingly and relentlessly away from what I had missed so much. The pain I felt that morning was something different than the dull rage and bitter gall that had been festering in me that autumn, much sharper than the bruised ache of sadness. This was a wound open and real and without guile and without Mama, I had no way to make it stop hurting. I lay in my bed for a while that morning, crying into my pillow until I rose to make the fires and start the day.

By the time I had dressed and gone to the kitchen to begin my rounds, my mind was clear and I knew I had chosen to stay. I would tell the madam later that very morning.

Chapter XIII

Charity Begins at Home

O nce my decision was made, I felt lighter. I even
worked up the nerve to ask Mrs. Hunt-Adams if
I could borrow a few books from the library for my
studies. She acquiesced without demur, happy with
me, I think, for having chosen to stay. I chose *Plato's
Dialogues* and a dictionary for starters and applied
myself to them both when I could. Ever since my
dream of Mama holding me, I tried in vain to dream
her again. I desperately missed the feeling I had in that
dream—safe. And something else—relaxed. Someone else was at the reins, in control. I didn't have to
do it all. At thirteen, my life was my own to make of
as I wished and I had voluntarily chosen service over
schooling, at least for a few more years.

Cook entrusted me more and more with errands
outside of the house and despite the cold, I loved
being about town. The owners of the market stalls
were mostly old friends and faces I'd grown up with.
The houses of the wealthy, to which I was regularly

sent with a note or package of some sort from the madam, were so elegant and alien from the outside that I could only feel awe for the accomplishment of living in such a mansion. But the kitchen doors, to which I, as a tweeny, gained entrance were remarkably similar to Cook's, and into these I was welcomed and offered refreshment or a tidbit of news. One time, Lawton, the Hunt-Adams's driver, pulled up by me while I strode along High Street and offered me a ride. There was no one in the carriage; he was on his way out to the Clay estate to fetch the master, so I rode alongside him and marveled at the view sitting up so high on the driver's bench.

I was delivering charity baskets to various parishioners on Mrs. Hunt-Adams's orders. Many of the wealthier ladies did that, sent out household goods to those less fortunate whose need was great. Many families did not have enough food that winter as the crop had been left to ruin as people fled. Cook and I had packed these larders earlier in the week and there were all manner of food stuffs and candles and a bit of cloth and needles as well.

Lawton looked at my baskets and commented, "Good provisions, I see." I looked sharply at him, for something in his tone alerted me to some criticism implied in the mild words. He faced forward and did not look at me.

"Well, one of these is for the Sextons, who live down from the Gratz place. You know who I mean?"

"Seems like I might."

"They lost their mama and two children to the epidemic. The missus does this work as an act of charity."

"Looks to me you and Cook doing most of the work," Lawton commented mildly.

I frowned. My infatuation with the madam could hardly tolerate even oblique criticism. I didn't understand her, I barely knew her, but I worshiped her, magnetically drawn to the protection she offered me with her beauty and power and wealth. I was a chick under her wing and I felt she deserved my loyalty. In truth, I had a schoolgirl "crush" on her. Defensively, I replied, "What madam is doing is an act of mercy. She doesn't have to give to others but she does, she's that good, Lawton, that's all. She's plain good."

How to explain the conversation Lawton and I had that day, punctuated mostly by silence. I could actually feel the weight of some criticism hanging in the air between us, but I can't tell you how I sensed it. Lawton very pointedly said nothing, a conversational tactic that allowed my words to hang uneasily between us. Finally, I said, "Do you not think it a mercy to provide for those in need? Isn't that what Jesus teaches?"

"Oh for certain, Miss Cal, for certain," he said, and again I could feel some subtext in his words, but could not find it.

"Lawton, surely you believe in charity?" I persisted.

"They say," he paused, "they do say charity begins at home." We pulled to a stop to allow some boys and their hogs to pass at Main Cross. Usher's Theater, the pride of the town, which had closed for the fall out of respect for the city's grief, was set to reopen at Christmas. I watched the boys using long thin branches to guide the hogs. I took in Usher's and mused as to what the new play or concert would be, and I was making note of new things I could see from this height. But beneath all that, my mind was preoccupied with what felt like a puzzle Lawton was challenging me to solve.

"Yes," I said slowly, "of course it does. Charity must start at home or it's hypocrisy." I looked at him and he looked me straight in the eye as a man, not a slave, not a servant, but a man, a black man.

"I don't understand," I said, and he raised his eyebrows as if to show he heard me, but he did not help me out, just let me stew. We trotted along in silence for a few blocks. "Well, she's practicing charity here in her hometown, isn't she?" I said at last, but even before I finished speaking, what he meant flew into my head fully formed. Mrs. Hunt-Adams kept slaves—Lawton was one of them—and there was no mercy there, no charity. It struck me like a thunderbolt and I had to clutch myself a moment to take it in.

We continued along but he slowed our pace. "Are you saying…?" I began but Lawton interrupted me.

"Now let's get one thing straight right here, Miss Cal, I ain't saying anything."

"No," I agreed, then lapsed into silence to think how to put what I was trying to say. Finally, I stated simply, "Slavery is just so wrong."

He nodded but did not look at me. Soon we were at the area of town that people were starting to call

Gratz Park because of how lovely the grounds were and I climbed down, thanking him for the ride. With that, he turned his team around and headed up Main Street and out the Richmond Road to Ashland, Henry Clay's estate.

That conversation, as remarkable for what was not said as for what was, stayed with me, for it forced me to recognize, to admit, that although Lawton put on a happy face and a kind of quiet simplicity, he was neither happy nor simple. Far from it. Not everything can be taken at face value. No one and nothing seemed quite one-dimensional anymore. As hard as I tried to contain madam in a separate place than mere mortals, she too began to acquire clay feet. It was a disheartening time for me and no one was exempt from my eagle eye and swift judgment. Mama retained her purity because she had died; had she been alive—oh, I cannot even finish that sentence for the deep longing that springs up in me. A disagreeable time perhaps, but surely essential. Discerning the multi-layered, interwoven strands and swaths of color and texture that make up who we are is part of the business of adulthood. I had come to it earlier than most, but come to it I did.

The winter deepened and a heavy snow fell followed by a cold snap. Everyone kept within doors for a few days. I heard some of the Hunt-Adams children fussing and arguing fractiously from time to time that week. The first time one of their raised petulant voices could be heard behind the kitchen door, my face must have betrayed my interest and surprise. "'Tis none of your affair," Cook was quick to reprimand me and swiftly sent me, armed with bucket and brush, up to the top of the house to work on the stairs. Nonetheless the whiny pitch of their voices told me everything I thought I needed to know about them; certainly enough to despise them as indulged rich children who didn't value what they had.

But here, once again, being a Freethinker muddied the waters. Just as I was basking in the sweet honeyed light of self-satisfaction and smug superiority, I began to wonder if there was something missing that made those children sound that way. I longed to dismiss them but I found it hard to do. At times I argued with Mama in my mind, an unconscious imitation of the children on the other side of the door (not that I ever sounded petulant or whiny, heaven forbid!). But I would call her to task for teaching me to question everything, to think for myself, to mine own self be true. Many a time, I would argue with her that it ill suited me for the world to have been taught to think the full of my thoughts.

And yet, as fervent, logical, and eloquent these internal protests were, I knew Mama—for all her non-conforming ways, for all the trouble my uncertainty brought me, for all the doubts I wrestled with—I knew she had been right to raise me as she did. She had treated me with such respect, and I'd learned somewhere along the way to respect myself. And if doing so made my life complicated, so be it.

Now, whenever I saw Lawton, for he often passed a few spare moments in Cook's warm, fragrant kitchen (never sitting down, of course, but a visit nonetheless), I was acutely aware that his easy-going, joshing exterior covered up an interior much more complex than I had known before. Lawton was a man for the horses. Kentucky was earning its reputation as the place to breed thoroughbreds. Henry Clay had set up the Racing Association. All the gentlemen belonged and the regular folk, both black and white, also participated if they could. Lexington was horse mad, my mother used to say. The races had been moved to a field outside of town, which was a relief from the days they would use Main Street as a track.

I can actually remember Mama almost being run down by stampeding horses. She must have been in her own world and paying no attention to her surroundings, and I, holding her hand, was following along on four- or five-year-old legs, hurrying and paying attention only to my predicament of how to keep up. A man grabbed her shoulders and with a loud, rude shout pulled us both back sharply. I fell over. At just that moment the horses thundered by, splashing us with mud and filling the air with the odors of sweat and leather and the thud of their hoofs and the cries from the riders, mere sounds, not words that I could tell. The man scolded Mama for her inattention and then apologized to both of us for being so rough. Mama thanked him for saving us and I never forgot my first taste of what they called "the sport of kings."

In fact, racing downtown had been illegal since late in the last century, but it still happened. The young men of town loved trying their horses out against each other and seemed unconcerned about the risks to passersby. And in truth, most people loved the races and willingly cleared the streets. Street boys would run up and down crying "Horse race two o'clock! Main Cross!" or whatever time and place it would start. Eventually, however, a tragic accident occurred and two citizens were actually trampled by the pack as the horses stampeded down the street.

This at last was too much for the City Fathers to tolerate. Henry Clay and Dr. Elisha Warfield came up with the idea of taking the races outside of town. Henry Clay also began breeding thoroughbreds, mixing Arabian stallions with Kentucky mares and he was reportedly delighted with the results. Apparently the bluegrass area sits on a great lot of limestone which makes the grass look blue and builds good bones, at least for horses. At any rate, Lexington was rapidly becoming a horse raising center of the whole country.

Lawton loved the races and where he got coin to gamble I do not know, but he would often relate his wins and losses and the incredible odds. Odds seemed a whole world in themselves requiring arithmetic skills I didn't have. Lawton could tell us the sire and dam of the horses he watched and their histories. I liked hearing him spin out the lineage of a horse and then discuss its legs, its hoofs, its lungs, its heart, even sometimes the horse's soul, which I am quite sure was anathema

126

to the church. Nonetheless, he knew these horses as if they were true friends or his own children. Only one time did I hear the same indefinable note in his voice I'd heard that day sitting with him as he drove the carriage. He was telling us about Senator Clay's thoroughbred barn. These barns were big and spacious and well heated, among the finest in the nation.

"Them horses are fed better than the slaves on his place," Lawton said offhandedly, but there it was again, that certain something that made me sit up and listen more closely. Henry Clay had a massive reputation in Lexington and for all I know throughout Kentucky and even the whole United States as a great man, a compromiser, a moderate force. I have heard him praised all my life. He said he agreed that slavery was wrong but he didn't think we should rush to end it as so many people depended on it. I had heard Mama and Aunt Charlotte discussing his stands many times. Both thought slavery should be best abolished sooner rather than later, but they could talk for hours about the problems that would come with abolition.

I have never had quite the esteem or regard for Senator Clay as other people in town. It stemmed from an incident in the Market House when I was about eight or nine. Mama and I were there doing a bit of shopping, a bit of visiting, as was much of the town. The Market House was covered from the rain by boards but open on the sides, and for women it was a common gathering place. Before Morton's Row went up, it was where everyone went for staples like flour or salt as well as other kinds of food stuffs. I was loitering about while Mama looked at buttons, when I saw a little girl who wasn't more than five. She was with her mama, a slave woman given a basket for groceries and sent to buy. But what riveted me, what paralyzed me with horror was a brand on the little girl's back. "HC" rose from her badly blistered and burned skin on her left shoulder. The skin was puffy and oozing, the brand glistened ugly and weeping on her skin.

It looked like a painful burn, but the child, beyond having taken her shirt off to relieve the pressure, did not seem to be in overmuch pain. I felt light-headed and dizzy all at once and may have staggered a step or two. The sight was disgusting, the practice outrageous, yet everyone, except me, went about their business with no more than a glance. The girl felt my stare on her and turned and smiled. Reflexively, I smiled back.

Henry Clay branded all of his slaves so that should they try to escape they would forever and always be identified as his property. Many men branded their slaves. It was common practice but for Henry Clay to do so and at the same time call slavery an abomination seemed the height of hypocrisy to me. He even said once that although he could clearly see the practical benefits of slavery (to him and others of his kind) he could never reconcile the fact that he knew it was morally wrong to own another person. I had a hard time understanding how he could walk such a crooked path. I guess when I know something's wrong, I quit doing it. I don't mean to sound holier than thou, but honestly my conscience pesters me to the point it's mostly easier just to be good. I guess Senator Clay tolerated his guilt better than I did.

So although the senator was one of our most celebrated and beloved citizens, after that day, seeing that child, I could never feel good about him. This actually brought me a bit of trouble with King who basically worshiped the senator. They had been born on the same plantation, in Hanover County, Virginia, and although King was the son of a servant and Henry Clay the son of the house, King's loyalty knew no bounds. Back when he had owned a bit of property, King voted for Clay at every opportunity. Once he was bribed with a flask of whiskey to vote for Clay's opponent. He voted for Clay, of course, and laughed about it for years to come. "Can't nobody tell me how to vote," he said, "though I sure do like it when they try."

So Henry Clay was not a hero of mine, but I had grown quite used to hearing his qualities lauded and had learned not to argue. After all, I was still a child in most people's eyes and had learned to hold my tongue—well, for the most part. So when Lawton said Henry Clay's thoroughbreds were fed better than his slaves I could not only well believe it, I condemned him for it. "What a shame, what a disgrace," I blurted out. This earned me a stern look from Cook and a quick glance from Lawton but nothing more was said by any of us.

That year, not six months after the cholera had killed so many, no one wanted to make too much merriment out of the Christmas holiday. I wanted no part of Christmas as it made the pain I carried around inside of me much sharper, remembering only the year before with Jackie newly born and Mama tired but happy and Pa gone off somewhere for a job or a drink or whatever—leaving us in peace. What a long way I had come in the year since then. What I didn't realize that year, as Christmas approached, was how much more change was yet to come.

Chapter XIV

Lawton

I was sitting at the kitchen table cracking nuts for Cook's cakes when I heard Missy scream. Cook's eyes met mine; we had both heard some special order of terror, despair, outrage in her cries. I jumped up and before Cook could say anything I was out the door and running toward the slave quarters. Missy was in the door of her cabin and the master was standing behind her. She had stopped screaming. I stopped running, trying to assess the situation. Master said something to Missy and then shouted something. I couldn't hear his words but Missy had quieted and now she hung her head. The master came further into the lane, looked back at her, spat in the dirt, and stomped up toward the front of the house, which to my relief took him up a different path from where I'd been standing, frozen.

Missy had disappeared back into the cabin and I ran to her. As I entered, a stench of blood and bowel and something else filled the air. I gasped as I took in what lay on the cot. Lawton's body was a flayed and bloody mess with skin flapping, bone protruding, even some of his guts spilled out. Most awful of all, though, was that there was still life in him. He wasn't recognizable by face, one cheek and eye were torn out, his mouth had been smashed in and a few bloody teeth could be seen within.

Missy knelt by his head. She had a warm wet cloth and she was trying to wipe some of the blood away. It was a fruitless task. "Oh, Lawton," I cried, dropping beside Missy and gazing, sickened but unable to look away from the wreck of his body. "What happened?" I asked.

Missy said low, "He ran away last night. The master sent the dogs and then they dragged him back here behind their horses." Tears rolled down her cheeks and her voice caught in a strangled sob as she uttered this dreadful news. She had stopped trying to clean the blood when skin came away as she wiped. She handed me her rag and I gently lifted and pushed a bit of intestine back into his stomach.

And then, my eye caught Lawton's remaining one. It was open and he was in there. It is a moment that haunts me and I expect to carry it with me to my grave. He was not defeated, just dying. He knew this was the risk—all the slaves knew this—but he wanted freedom so badly he was willing to risk it. Suddenly I knew what I should do. I stood up and told Missy, "I'm going for Aunt Charlotte." And with that I stepped out of the cabin into the momentarily mild December afternoon. I ran back into the kitchen, told Cook briefly what happened, ran upstairs to get my cloak, and without asking permission, said as I entered the kitchen, "I'm going down to Second Creek to fetch Aunt Charlotte."

I saw my unfinished mound of nuts and added, "I'll finish those soon as I can." Cook never said a word, or if she did I didn't hear it. She just stared at me with a look I thought might be condemning. My legs began to move and I flew down the hill with a terrible keen awareness of having made this same desperate dash on June 1st. I tried to keep the pictures of Lawton being attacked by dogs and dragged by horses out of my mind, but could only come up with Mama and Jackie dying in filth instead. There was no way out of my mind, nothing to do but run, and that I could do and did.

I burst in on Aunt Charlotte who was toasting her toes on a bumper round her hearth, and startled her out of a nap. Quickly, I explained. She blanched when I described Lawton's condition but sat right up, and began to reach for her shoes. "First, go get yourself a drink of that cider; you're about to burn up, even in this cold. Then go harness Abel, and if you see King, tell him where we're going." With that she heaved herself up and went through to the curtained side of the room where she kept her remedies. I took a long swallow of her cider and felt my feet steady beneath me. I grabbed a biscuit too and rushed to the shed behind her house that served as Abel's barn. In no time, although it seemed forever, we were headed out of the creek, into town and up on the Hill. It was still daylight but moving on toward evening. As we pulled

133

in, Thomas, Jimmy's husband, met us. He was solemn and wordless as he helped Aunt Charlotte down. I searched his face for answers but could not read what I saw there.

Lawton was still alive when Aunt Charlotte came to him. Missy and Jimmy were sitting with him but not touching him as there was no part on his body that wasn't raw. He moaned softly in a helpless way that rent our hearts.

Aunt Charlotte sat down with ponderous care on the stool that Missy brought. She crooned to Lawton, not words that I could make out, just soothing sounds of comfort. She turned to me and instructed me to boil water. There was a kettle on the hearth so my real job was to find a bowl to put water in. I knew she was making a concoction of some sort, but I couldn't imagine which of her herbs and barks could help him.

When I brought her the bowl of hot water, she sent me again to get a spoon. There was only a carved wooden one so I brought that. Aunt Charlotte mixed and mashed various roots and dried flowers. She didn't instruct me as she usually did when she was doctoring. She continued the soft blanketing talk, all of it nonsense but comforting nonetheless. The only other sound in the cabin was the wheezing whistling sound of Lawton's chest or what was left of it under the bloody ribbons of his shirt. He had clearly been whipped in addition to being savaged by dogs and dragged in the dirt for how many miles. "You gonna be just fine now, Lawton," Aunt Charlotte soothed him. She dipped the spoon into the bowl and dribbled a little into his smashed mouth. He struggled to swallow and somehow managed. She poured a few more drops. This tedious painful process continued until Lawton's good eye closed and he went to sleep.

We sat there in mournful silence, all four of us watching Lawton sleep. Eventually Missy and Jimmy went to Jimmy's cabin to fix something to eat. Aunt Charlotte and I continued our vigil. "This a bad business," she said at last in a low growly voice.

It had been quiet for so long I startled a little when she spoke, but I answered with what was in my heart. "Aunt Charlotte, this is worse than a bad business, this is murder." I realized when I spoke the words that I knew Lawton was dying, had been all along as we sat there. Aunt Charlotte was helping him out. She'd doctored him so he wouldn't have to feel what they'd done to his body.

"Honey," she said now, sounding infinitely old, "you know well as I do a rich white man like Mr. Hunt-Adams can't murder a black slave. It's in the law."

Well, it's a bad law is what I wanted to say, but I thought it would make me seem childish and just then I felt anything but. I knew she was right. Even if it wasn't law, the differences in their stations made Mr. Hunt-Adams invincible. Lawton was a disposable person. Not to me who was his friend. Not to Missy or Thomas or Jimmy who were his family. Not to his cousins and nephews and nieces. To us, Lawton was real, smart and funny and kind and so desperate to be free

135

he gave his life for the attempt. I felt exhaustion seep suddenly into my bones but I didn't want to leave him.

We lapsed back into silence. Aunt Charlotte lit her pipe and rocked slowly on her stool, propping her back up against the wall. After maybe an hour, more or less—I cannot describe the hours of that day, there were far too many of them. But slowly, the way Lawton was breathing changed. It became longer and longer between each faint rise of his ruined chest, and the sound of it was different as well, although I can't quite explain how.

"It won't be long now," Aunt Charlotte said, and I realized she was speaking to Lawton, not to me. "Soon enough, dear friend, soon enough." She began to hum a hymn that I recognized but didn't know the words to. And along about the third time through, Lawton quit breathing and died.

For a moment the room was startlingly silent without Lawton's gasping breaths and Aunt Charlotte and I just sat with him for a few terrible minutes. Then she said, "Honey, I need you to go tell Jimmy and the others that he's passed over." I hated spreading such awful news. Weeping and wailing arose as Lawton's family and a few others gathered in the small shack to say their goodbyes. What a horrible unjust death Lawton had endured. I too wept bitter, angry tears and although I felt like screaming as some were doing, I was unable to let myself go.

Later the women would wash his mutilated body and prepare him for burial. We had gathered in the common area to honor Lawton and to comfort each other. He was well liked and well respected, and as word spread, slaves from nearby mansions came by too. Suddenly, into this scene stormed Mr. Hunt-Adams. "Break this up, damn you. All of you," he shouted. He was florid and inflamed, obviously enraged. The cries stopped and the yard was quiet. "Lawton served this family for forty some years and this is the gratitude he shows. He ran away from me, and it's going to cost a goodly sum to buy another. No loyalty, no gratitude." It was a vicious, ugly, and ridiculous accusation that Lawton didn't display gratitude for his enslavement. No one spoke or even breathed. He shouted, "Now shut up before I make you shut up." Then he was gone as quickly as he'd come. I watched him head up the path and then, on the veranda I saw Mrs. Hunt-Adams, clutching her cloak and looking pale and distressed.

Inside there followed a deep, hurt silence that ended when Jimmy raised her voice in song and we all joined in singing "Abide with Me." After that, they sang some songs I didn't know but I hummed along anyway. The singing brought us some peace and eventually the men and children went to the other cabin and just the women remained. Aunt Charlotte told me to go and get some sleep, for I would need my strength for tomorrow.

I obeyed, leaving Missy and Jimmy and Aunt Charlotte to clean him and sit with him through the night. It was at least midnight when I went into the kitchen. I saw Cook had left me a plate of beans and bread with a bite of pork but my stomach rebelled. Leadenly I walked up

137

to our attic bedroom. To my surprise Mrs. Alice was awake. Not only awake but sitting in our single chair, reading by candlelight. She was waiting for me.

I stumbled when I saw her, and she stood up to catch me. I hugged her hard and she hugged me back with a strength that amazed me. I started to cry but she shook her head and closed her eyes. She put her finger to her lips not to silence me, to get me to talk. "Tell?" I guessed, and she smiled.

So I did. I tried to be quiet to keep us out of trouble, but my voice rose several times. I told her how Lawton looked, how much he was hurt and how Aunt Charlotte had eased his pain. I explained how Mr. Hunt-Adams had stomped down there to his slaves' quarters to yell at them for mourning a man he had murdered. I explained it all and even though I cried a few times in the telling, she didn't stop me again. At the end we just sat there, I on my bed, she on the chair. Really, what could be said in reply to this awful night, so I got ready for bed.

I was as tired as I can ever remember being, but that night, before we blew out the candle, I told Mrs. Alice goodbye. She looked sad but she nodded her understanding. The next morning I was up as usual before the house. That day, however, I did not clean the ashes and start their fires, nor did I fetch water nor did I do even one of my dozens of tasks. Instead, I wrote a note telling Cook goodbye. I was done with them. I had no idea what to do next but I knew for certain I couldn't live there any longer.

King had come by sometime during the night with

a simple coffin he had hammered together for Lawton. Even this early there were other blacks, both free and slave, coming by to pay their respects. In the one part of town where most of the free blacks lived, there was a preacher, Brother Moses Fisher, who would give Lawton a funeral. It would be abbreviated, for sure, as Mr. Hunt-Adams would have stopped it if he'd known, but he never did.

Early that morning, Christmas Eve morning it was, King wheeled his cart downtown and we followed, Thomas and Missy and I as well as Eli on foot and Aunt Charlotte and Jimmy in her wagon. The ground was too hard to bury him but Lawton's body would be kept in the church shed till thaw. We gathered in the Black Baptist Church which was no more than a single room. There was a great deal of crying and weeping and sighing and singing. But it was quick. Preacher Fisher said his words and we said ours and then we had to leave him and scurry back to our places.

Except that I no longer had a place, not any place I wanted. The note I left on Cook's table said I quit. Mrs. Hunt-Adams would get no notice. I was as free as a bird with nowhere to go and no one to care. I knew as soon as I thought such a thing it was melodramatic and self-pitying. I chided myself to be fair and then, as though I had thought through all my options and knew exactly what to do, I simply turned my boots toward Third Street and Broadway to the Orphan Asylum where I asked if they had room and they said they did.

Chapter XV

Melancholia

Thus it was I ushered in the year 1834, as well as my fourteenth birthday. I was as low and sad as I have ever been; it was as though Lawton's death brought Mama and Jackie's deaths roaring back. I even grieved for my father and I became sick with grief. I didn't know it then but I have learned since that every hurt brings back the others you have suffered through. I was weary and so sad, having been tossed about like a cork on the sea. Most of all I was lonely.

The Orphan Asylum is off Broadway, on Hampton Court, the newest school in town. Mama and Pa both wanted me to be educated and now I wanted that too. I had buried both my parents last year and my baby brother. I will always have a piece of them in me. Mama will always be telling me to write and Pa will always be sticking up for the poor and losing his temper. In my mind his arms are always swinging. He was a dangerous man, but my Pa nonetheless, and I confess I loved him. Is everyone as mixed up as I am about their parents? Jackie was just himself: sweet, innocent, young and pure, now gone but somehow still present for me, still in me. Such a loss to the world. I spent that first night in my new bed, wetting the sheet with my tears. I thanked Mama for bequeathing me the full of my thoughts. They are plenty to keep me busy.

The new year began quietly, the Home was not yet officially open so the building was very quiet. I was put to bed and made to rest for a week. A week! Can you believe it? A whole week in bed, but in fact I mostly slept through it. I think my illness was in my heart more than my body but sleep did help and, of course, as I learn and learn again, so did having work to do.

Matron was a large doughy woman whose breasts seemed to steer her body, like the prow of a ship. She wore a white apron and kept her keys on her waist. I was given a bed and a box in which to keep my things, and most wonderful of all, a desk with a chair. I had never had one of those and it made me feel important, as though my writing was important enough to have a piece of furniture all its own. A fanciful notion, I know, but fancies have always helped me through.

All the children who came were expected to get an education, not just the boys. The women who opened the Home are forward thinking enough to consider we girls needed educating as well as the boys. I know people think at fourteen you are still a child but I didn't feel much like one. I felt old and tired.

I didn't know when the other children would arrive, but in the meantime it was just Matron, a little boy named Timmy, and me. The rooms smelled like fresh wood and paint. Everything was so new and clean I felt timid at first about doing anything. I'd never lived in someplace so new and shiny. I guess our little house was new when Pa finished building it but I was a baby then and don't remember.

Timmy is only five so he sleeps in with Matron. After my first few days asleep, I woke up and felt able to help with the work of getting the place ready. My birthday seemed a terrible day to me. No one knew and no one cared that I would be turning another year in this world. King and I shared the day, but he was probably off somewhere drinking and cutting a shine.

As I woke on January 1st, 1834, I felt a deep and hollow emptiness. My feet dragged and I kept my eyes down. I know self-pity is an ugly thing but that was what I felt. But I should have known I wasn't forgotten by everyone because who should show up that day in the afternoon but Aunt Charlotte. She brought me a delicious slice of her famous walnut and honey cake.

"Aunt Charlotte, you shouldn't have come out in this cold," I exclaimed when I saw her. Truth to tell, she didn't look quite well, or maybe I was just noticing the new lines around her eyes and mouth.

"Well, baby, I wanted to bring you something for your birthday. Can it be true you're already fourteen?"

"Yes, ma'am, you know I am," I laughed, remembering all of the tales she and Mama used to tell about the day I was born.

"Still scrawny, child. Your blessed mama would want

me to fatten you up a mite," she said, and with that she produced that slice of her delicious cake. I was touched to tears, something that still happens with regularity to me. I could feel them aching up and pouring out of my eyes, all without my consent.

"Thank you," I mumbled. I hugged her and she held me for a few moments in her arms. When I pulled away, I said, "How can you smell like lavender in January?"

She laughed and said, "I've got my ways, Cal, I've got my ways." Out of her pocket she pulled a sachet. It was made of plain linsey woolsey, but filled with dried lavender and rose petals. She scrunched it up and held it under my nose. The sachet was for my clothes, to keep them smelling sweet until spring came.

Matron knew Aunt Charlotte and gave her a cup of tea. I suppose almost everyone in town knows Aunt Charlotte because of her doctoring and owning a horse and buggy, both technically illegal for a black woman. And of course, she is also renowned for being the only black woman who ever "owned" a white man. King's indenture was almost up but the story made for good telling and soon grew legs. He used to be ridiculed as the town drunk but was now given new respect having buried half this town's loved ones.

King and I were friends before he got famous but I was glad to see him getting some respect. Besides being born on the same day, the two of us just get along. Aunt Charlotte had bought our family house on Second Creek after the city auctioned it off to pay back taxes. King was living there now and had been since the end of the epidemic. Aunt Charlotte also got her stall back at the New Market and had found a girl to help her. I thought this time last year I would be that girl, but here I am instead.

Matron let me walk outside with Aunt Charlotte when she left. I took a sugar cube out to Abel. He was a swayback old fellow but sturdy and faithful. "It's lonely here now, sweetie," Aunt Charlotte said, "but it won't stay that way. You'll see. Be a good girl and say your prayers," she counseled.

"Yes, ma'am," I answered obediently, although my praying comes and goes. "Oh, Aunt Charlotte, I don't know if I'm going to make it sometimes. I get so down-hearted."

"I know, baby, I know."

"What should I do?" I asked, feeling desperate all of a sudden. She seemed to understand because she took both my hands between hers to calm me.

"We'll just hold hands and go on," she said. "It'll be all right by and by. You'll see."

I promised I would come and see her when I had time, then I stood on the street and watched as she drove her little cart away.

Chapter XVI

The Orphan Asylum

O nce I got over being so tired, Matron put to me work making up rooms for the incoming orphans. The second week we had twenty-five arrive. There was a good deal of crying and carrying on among the little ones. Perhaps it was one change too much for some of them. I knew a few of them, little Ellis Dickens, from down the creek. He was the only one of his family to survive. I did what I could to give comfort, but there was a limit to what I had to give. I know how selfish that sounds, but it is true nonetheless. I was stretched inside and could not breathe very well sometimes. When the little ones started crying, it made it that much harder.

I shared a room with a girl called Sylvie. I didn't know her before, her family lived up beyond the Old Parker Mill. Sylvie was my age, actually a few months older, and we were the oldest female orphans in the Home. She was missing a tooth right up in the front of her mouth that made her look a little frightening at

147

first, but she seemed a gentle enough soul. Sylvie's family was not all destroyed by the cholera but her mama was. Sylvie and her two younger brothers had come to stay while her pa headed out West, to find some place far from Lexington for them to start over. He said he would come back to claim them when the time was right.

At supper, Matron had us stand at the table before we sat and pray thanks for our food. Many nights we had potatoes and onions with milk and bread. The big room was oddly quiet for there to be so many children. Matron said there would be more to come. When the teacher Miss Teaberry came, it was a measure of relief. I knew she would help to set things to rights. Really, the number of children that started pouring into the Home was staggering. The older ones helped the younger ones and it worked pretty well, but I think we all wanted someone to take charge. Of course, I see it plain, we all wanted a mother, and why wouldn't we? Almost everyone had lost at least a mother and most, like me, had lost much more. Loss was nothing of note at the Orphan Asylum.

Since Sylvie and I were the oldest ones we were called on a great deal to comfort and cajole and care for the ones who needed a little extra loving or patting on. I had to pull a tooth one day, it was for a little girl named Sally. It was wobbling something fierce but she couldn't bring herself to pull it so it came to me. Yank. Ouch. And then a hug.

At the Orphan Asylum, we all had to work to pay

for our board. At the end of the day, I would be black with ashes and weary with fatigue from helping with the fires. "Fatigue" means tired in both French and English, which makes it a very clever word. It was truly filthy work and made me cough something awful. Good thing we all got extra baths. Matron was firm about keeping us clean. For me it meant a lot of fetching water which is back-breaking work. Matron had a naval husband or father, I am not sure which, but when there was work to be done she would call, "Line up, boys and girls, time to swab the decks!" and we would get busy with whatever task she had assigned us. I was put to work in the laundry too, since I had experience there from the Hunt-Adams house. The orphans' clothes were easier since there were no fine materials to worry about. We all wore the plainest cotton shifts and linens. Almost all of the servants were slaves. I felt quite odd at times, having been a servant myself, although never a slave. It changes the way I look at things around me.

One day, Sylvie and I got a new "roommate," Josephine, a raven-haired little elf of a girl with slanting oval eyes. She carried with her an aura of restraint. The three of us had not much trouble adjusting to each other's ways. She was a noisy sleeper, however, but except for her giggles and moans and yells and whispers, there were no real problems. She was only eight but a very dignified eight.

When I had the time, I employed my beautiful desk, writing in a notebook Matron had found for me. I felt very close to Mama as I sat searching for words and dreaming back to the days before the flood swept my life away. I could get lost in my memories and Mama was right that putting thoughts into words made them clearer. I began to not only think the full of my thoughts but write them too. One day Sylvie wanted to know what I was writing and I told her it was the history of my life so far. She nodded. We all have our histories now, all us orphans have been through much.

On Sundays, we went to Christ Church Episcopal. Even though God and I have had our falling out, the organ was beautiful and brought tears to my eyes. The sound was not only large it was deep and full and made my heart swell. And the stained glass was so intricate and finely done. Scenes from the Bible were depicted and I enjoyed looking at them as I listened to the minister drone on. Sundays we had chicken dinner with mashed potatoes and peas. And best of all, there was always some kind of sweet—apple crisp or white cake or sometimes iced berries. It made church worth getting through.

The ladies of the town provided for us from their farms. Mrs. Hunt-Adams brought us bushels of potatoes, which there can never be too much of. Waveland sent us a large batch of hemp that we made into clothes and rope and other needful things. And yes, they sent turnips enough to last the winter and then some. Mrs. Clay sent barrels of flour and of cider. She also sent cheese and beans and even some precious sugar.

The Clay farm, Ashland, was a wonder to behold.

Two years ago, Dame Holcomb took some of us to see it. We traveled in a buggy out the Richmond Road. The carriage ride was bumpy and exciting and we were all a bit wrought up, having been given the privilege to go. The lawn there was dappled with little white flowers called spring beauties. We were greeted and taken into the garden to have a cool drink. We were treated like royalty although we were just girls. A woman who is a cousin to Aunt Charlotte served us lemonade. Her name was Willie and she was a slave woman. I imagine she, like all of Henry Clay's slaves, had been branded, something hard for me to think on. Having seen that little girl, with her brand still weeping with pain and pus, I could not think of Great Harry as we were supposed to.

In our classroom at the orphanage, Miss Teaberry paired us up, the older with the younger, so that everybody, except for the littlest babies, had to help someone else. It was a fairly brilliant way to do it, frankly, because as we taught something, anything, we learned it all that more, and in this school we were all learning together. My group is mostly the eight-year-olds, like Josephine. Some can read and some cannot. Carla and Darla, our twins, had already started in on small words like "sit" and "dog" and "cat." I also was teaching them how to hold their pencils, although I must say it was fair different for the left-handed ones than the right-handed ones. It was a challenge for me to see the paper at the angle the lefties had to hold it, but in truth it is just another example of people being different and needing different things.

Under Miss Teaberry's guidance I started reading the Bible on my own. She exhorted me to read it slowly and thoughtfully, which was hard since God and I are having a bit of a rough period. Nonetheless there is much to be learned. Our family Bible was lost in the flood, but Mama had read it to me often, although always encouraging me to ask questions. At the Hunt-Adams's, I read the Bible under Cook's eye although she never asked me a thing, expecting me to accept it as the truth, as Gospel, as they say. At the Orphan Asylum we had a Bible in every room but not everyone took the time to read it.

Miss Teaberry had Sylvie and me sketching buildings and then using math to figure out angles and corners and degrees. It all gave me a headache. I found it tedious and hard, but I loved the sketching. Sylvie was really quite gifted at drawing, her buildings looked as they were supposed to, while mine did not. We drew the cow barn that was out back from the kitchens and Sylvie's was so good I could almost smell the straw and manure.

We had three sweet cows—May, June, and July—and they could not make enough milk for all of us, but they did the best they could. There is something calming in being with a cow. Their sweet ears are so soft and I loved to lay my cheek on their flank and just feel their heat.

I knew Mama would approve of Miss Teaberry's strictures and although I didn't always enjoy learning as much as I wished I would, I did respect her and wonder if someday I, too, might be a teacher. Of course it would mean never marrying, but at that age I didn't really care about marrying. Not after I saw what happened between Mama and Pa.

One day, I think it was in January, it snowed and snowed and then snowed some more. It was a wonderful white falling silence. What sounds there were came from afar: sleigh bells, a few hearty voices, dogs barking in excitement. For most of the day we stayed inside watching it come down, but when it finally stopped, around seven o'clock in the evening, we bigger girls held lanterns for the boys who shoveled out pathways. Someone started a sea chanty, "Heave ho and up she rises," and the rest of us picked it up. It had nothing to do with snow but it was lovely to hear our happy voices in the night. The trees hung with glistening folds of snow and it was a good feeling to have us working together and being glad while we did.

Some of the boys at the Asylum were nice and some were absolutely horrid. They probably thought the same of us girls and they'd be right. I had a small liking for Lucas Brown who came from Maysville, upriver where the flood started. His entire family on both sides died from cholera in a mere two-day period. We were introduced after church one Sunday because Sylvie knew his cousin, Paul. We boys and girls were kept separated for most things except for school, but that was what made the night of the big snow so special. We got to work together.

Lucas has big brown eyes and the biggest ears

153

I've ever seen. That might not sound like a wonderful feature but he wore them well. Like most us, his smile was a little sad and all in all I felt myself falling soft for him. That night we sent teases back and forth between us, the boys and the girls. Soon the boys started shoveling even faster and we girls cheered them on until they started throwing snow at us.

Matron must have heard too much merriment in our voices because she ordered us inside. I was sent to put the little ones to bed. Josephine touched my cold cheeks with her little hands and laughed when I started shaking the snow from me like a big dog. That night it felt good to curl up in bed in our warm quilts and blankets. We orphans held together and it made us feel safer. Our asylum that night felt real.

One day King came by to let me know Aunt Charlotte was warm and snug in her house. The city was mostly closed down in that weather but King could go wherever he wanted. He just made his way. I obviously had no cigar stubs for him but gave him apples instead. His cheeks burned red but I think the whiskey kept him warm. I gave him a hug and felt good to be wrapped in that boozy embrace.

A doctor named Dr. Rank and two others whose names I misremember set up a clinic for the orphan children. This was a charity clinic, they got nothing for their time but our gratitude and more to the point, perhaps, they got their wives' approval. I knew from my days as a tweeny that when the lady of the house wants something done, it was done. And these ladies, the "quality" some call them (although not I), wanted us orphans cared for.

My great fortune was that I was chosen to assist the doctors. Most of the children we saw suffered chilblains, earache, and cough. Several heads were shaved to contain galloping cases of lice. I can only thank my stars I never caught them. I dripped warm oil into aching ears and spooned honey and cider down many a throat. I wished Aunt Charlotte could be there because her herbs and simples had helped many for years, but the doctors disdained her remedies and would never let a black woman into the clinic besides.

But even I, who don't know much, knew that warmer rooms, heavier clothes, and better food were most of what these children needed. To be truthful, what they needed was a family. Sometimes the doctors spoke in Latin or arcane phrases I could not understand. Naturally they didn't stoop to explain it to the likes of me, but it made me want to know more. I liked helping in the clinic and could see that maybe one day I could find a way to make a living helping others.

Lexington began to grow outward toward the Orphan Asylum. All around us there were building projects. Within a few months we were no longer the only building on our "block," as the city engineers were calling the plots they laid out. Streets and buildings were being planned. We saw engineers and architects pacing the lots, and the master carpenters were everywhere. Even though it was the dead of winter, it no longer felt like it. Merchants had moved up town to serve not only the orphans but the many people living out there now.

Being one of the older girls, I was often sent on errands. One day I was sent with a message to the Hunt-Adamses. Oh, what a pleasure it was to see Cook, and Mrs. Alice came flying up the steps from the basement like she could hear me, which she couldn't if she's deaf, but there she was. Not only that, she was smiling. I reached over and hugged her and she shut her eyes until I let go. She made out like I had grown, which is not much true but undoubtedly I had changed in just those few weeks.

I truly do not understand how life can be so full and deep and pointed and painful and altogether incredible every single day. I don't know why people don't age quicker than they do. Personally, I feel overcome by the pace and magnitude of changes in my life. I wonder if others feel as I do—that sometimes it's all a bit much. I know Mama would say I am indulging my imagination, which is probably true, but it was less than a year ago I was living on Second Creek with Mama and Jackie, then I became a tweeny and learned the life of the "quality" from the inside. In April, King told me Pa had been killed in a fight. And in June, Mama and Jackie died, and later, during that siege of a summer, baby Rose was spirited away in a way that broke my heart, and at Christmastime Lawton was murdered for wanting his freedom. I suppose I should be rejoicing that I am alive and take heart that I will see them all someday in Heaven, but in fact, I am not a Christian. I just don't believe we'll all be dancing in the clouds and playing harps and having a great death being so close to God.

Mama was a Christian but she was also a Free-thinker and was training me up to be one too. I've always had to think things through for myself and Heaven is a step too far for me. Maybe it's my melancholy nature or just my plain grumpiness but I can't believe in God the Father, the Son, and the Holy Ghost. Lord alone knows what Miss Teaberry or Matron or Mrs. Hunt-Adams would say. I don't think Aunt Charlotte would be overly bothered by it, but still a person can't just say she's not a Christian. Christians don't take it lightly, at least in my experience.

On February 14th, Lucas, the boy I had taken a shine to, gave me a piece of candy. It was wrapped in the prettiest paper I had ever seen, colored red and silver, absolutely beautiful. He came out of line to see me when we were walking out to the grounds for work duty. "Hey, Cal," he said, "this is for you." Quick as that he put the candy in my hand and fell back into line heading for the barn. I couldn't stop smiling. Sylvie teased me something awful but it just made me laugh. He likes me for sure. I never thought much about Valentine's Day before, but I don't think I'll forget it now.

At the orphanage, we celebrated holidays by singing. On George Washington's birthday, before luncheon, we sang "My Country 'Tis of Thee" in his honor. One of the ladies had donated a piano to our home and Matron pounded out the notes. Singing that song pinched me a little as I remembered my disappointment at not being able to sing it for President Jackson. My parents were both dedicated to the belief that it is a privilege to be an American, that we are a frontier generation in the frontier of this nation. Both my grandfathers fought in the Revolution and lived to tell of it. My pa told how the people were so grateful to Washington for winning the war they offered to make him King. Washington wouldn't do it, Pa said, because this is a democracy, in which we don't have kings, we elect our representatives, including our President.

My pa was a man of contradictions. He could be terribly mean at times. But he was also a man who stood up against slavery and I have to respect that. I did not like the contradictions. So often I had wished he could be one thing or another, plain, simple, but he is—I mean, was—not that way. Well, the sad thing is that since he is dead now, all I have left are my memories, which are unsure at best. He can't add word one to the discussion. It's funny how holidays at the orphanage remind me of people I have lost and miss. (Maybe that's the holy part of holiday.)

Chapter XVII

Aunt Charlotte's Gift

I hid out in the orchard one Sunday from early light on to keep from going to church or seeing people. I wanted badly to be alone. I felt strange and unbalanced, like I might scream or talk in whispers, that I might rave or drool or cry. Being in with the trees all day was good for me; even in the dead of winter there are a surprising number of things living and growing in the orchard. There were some old apples from the previous fall on the ground and I nibbled around the wormholes and the rotten spots to eat a few mealy bites. A part of me was wild that day and wanted to howl at the sky, the moon, and the stars. This still happens to me from time to time, when I need to be away from everyone.

When I went back I found out no one had really missed me. That was a relief but it also felt sad. Sylvie had a pass to go visit with her father's brother. I was glad (and a little envious) she had some family left and prospects to look forward to. I am a real and true orphan since not only are both my parents dead so are all their kin. There is no other family for me, except Aunt Charlotte, but no one would countenance a white girl living with a black woman. Even her ability to flaunt the race laws would not be powerful enough to overcome that prejudice. I remember wishing one day I could be judged apart from my parents, my family. Now, how tragically true it has become. I will be known as myself, Calendula Farmer—Cal, to most people. And only those who knew my parents will remember them. I guess the old saw "Be careful what you wish for, it might come true," has some truth to it.

I needed time to think is how I explained it to Matron upon my return. Well, I've been doing my thinking with my hands busy, which is Matron's solution to everything. I am being given extra work because she did miss me when I was hiding out, and she doesn't want me "to disappear like that again."

"Cal," Matron said and leveled her gaze to mine, "we all need to get away sometimes, and I understand how a young woman your age might need some time to herself, but it is wrong to let down people who are counting on you,"

"Yes, ma'am," I said, feeling she really had a point. She called me a "woman." Me? I don't think so.

"Who are the people you let down?" she went on. "Have you thought about them?"

Actually I hadn't much. "No, ma'am," I said quietly, "I just needed to get away."

"So you were thinking of yourself," Matron said.

"Yes, ma'am."

She looked at me for a long moment. I was too humiliated to look at her, but when she spoke there was a tone of humor, not anger in her voice. "We must think of ourselves, Calendula. Just not to the exclusion of everyone else. Do you understand?"

"I think so, ma'am."

"Well, you think about it some more while you are working in the garden this spring."

"Yes, ma'am." She still did not rise to end our interview, and I was fair burning with embarrassment and shame.

"Cal, next time you need time off, just ask."

I looked up to see if she meant it and she gave me a smile.

"Thank you, Matron," I said, smiling back at her.

She missed me! I thought that was rather amazing. And even though she seemed to have forgiven me completely, I knew it was wrong to run and hide. But I'm still glad I had the time to myself.

You would think that living in a school building full of orphans, I would have felt some sympathy for someone other than myself, but I am not sure I really did. This was the worst of it. Grief had made me selfish. I could not explain it, but I suffered with the guilt of it nonetheless.

One day I heard that King had slipped somehow and broke a leg. He was staying at Aunt Charlotte's house until he healed. Poor old King. He was in a lot of pain and Aunt Charlotte's remedies didn't quite take the edge off. Testing Matron, I asked for permission to go visit them and she gave it. I went to see the two of them to catch up with their news.

"Whiskey is wonderful for whatever ails you, Cal," King told me, with a sideways grin at Aunt Charlotte. "The more you drink, the less pain you feel."

"Oh shut yer trap, old man," Aunt Charlotte said.

"I wish I could get her to add whiskey to her set of cures," he teased, winking at me.

King knows what she thinks about that. This is an old argument between them. "It would taste a sight better than that chamomile tea she pours down me," he continued.

"I'm getting ready to pour something really nasty down your throat if you don't quit yer yapping. What are you telling that girl?" Aunt Charlotte was mad or as mad as she ever got.

"Now, now," King said, real low and smiling, "let's all stay friends."

King's leg was healing and in general he seemed in good health, although being kept a good deal more sober than he would prefer. Aunt Charlotte fed him teas and potions, and bread and pie and good home cooking. King needs that after his whiskey binges. Every year he grows more wrinkled and battered and used, but he stays friendly and kind and gentle. I would have loved it if my own pa could have been a gentle drunk but he wasn't. But King, who is sort of like a grandpa to me, he is one gentle soul. I tried to cheer him up by giving news of the orphans who sent their

162

love. Like almost all the children in Lexington, we orphans adored King. What he really wanted was a bottle of whiskey and a good cigar, but I couldn't help him out there anymore.

They are an odd pair, King and Aunt Charlotte. Besides him being white and her being black, besides him being so dirt poor he was indentured to her, and her being well off or at least comfortable enough to "buy" him, besides him being a drunk and her being a healer—well, besides all that, they are both my friends and more or less the only family I can really call mine. I also think the two of them are more to each other than they show the world. Which is wise.

School progressed and I did too. I admired Miss Teaberry tremendously, and I learned things every day in my lessons, something that didn't always happen at Dame Holcomb's. Yesterday, I read a discourse on electricity written by the honorable Benjamin Franklin himself. It will take many more readings before the meaning will come clear. I'm a slow learner but steady. Miss Teaberry is infinitely patient and doesn't get angry, no matter how stupid my question or wrong my answer. I try to imitate her when I work with the little ones, but there are plenty of times I raise my voice. I wonder if that's Pa coming out in me and hope not.

The Orphan Asylum is a place where everyone works. There is no choice about that. This puts work in a different position than it has in the "outside" world.

What I know, from working at the Hunt-Adams's, is that some people are so rich they don't have to work. What I know from living my life is that I am not one of them.

I no longer wanted to be like Mrs. Hunt-Adams. Ever since Lawton died, I had remembered her hand clasped to her mouth, her color paling, her big eyes growing bigger. I knew she, as the master's wife, had no say of her own, no property, no voice, certainly no vote. And yet, I held her to blame as well. If I ever would forgive her, I would never again want to be her. I had these imaginings in my mind of Mrs. Hunt- Adams calling my name and talking to me in her low honeyed voice. I would imagine she wanted to tell me she is against slavery, but I could not look her in the imaginary eye. I did not want to be around her anymore.

Spring came again. Little flowers popped up everywhere. We planted peas and onions in the kitchen garden. Sylvie and I took four of the little ones— Carla, Darla, Josephine, and Billy—and went to collect greens. My mama was a big one for greens and Matron liked them well enough. The greens just grew for the having and we ate plenty of them.

We were collecting dandelion leaves and looking for four-leaf clovers when we saw Lucas leading Clyde, the Orphan Asylum's horse, into the barn. Lucas flashed me a grin. I gave him back a little smile, then ducked my head while I felt my skin go bright red and fiery hot. We didn't say a word, but still, it was like volumes were spoken between us. Sylvie teased me no end for the rest of the day, but I really don't mind. I do like him.

Aunt Charlotte came knocking at the door, right after breakfast. I was still in the kitchen, washing out and drying pans. She had come to see me, and Matron said when I finished my job, we could have a visit. Sylvie helped me wipe so I was done in no time. Aunt Charlotte took a hold of my arm and walked me back out to the street where her buggy was parked. Abel was tied to the post and waiting. Just as I began searching my pockets for a carrot or piece of apple, Aunt Charlotte handed me a sugar cube. Abel's warm snuffling lips took the sugar from the flat palm of my hand. I petted his velvety smooth nose and looked into his big brown eyes. Abel is such a good horse.

Aunt Charlotte went around to the buggy and lifted out a large flat tray with plants on it. She put it on the ground. "Come here, Cal," she directed. "This is your name flower. I wanted you to have some." I must have looked as confused as I felt. "This is a calendula, Cal," she explained, "the flower you are named after."

I looked down at the plants at my feet. At first I could see only the green of the leaves mixed with the dark mud of the dirt they were in. As I looked closer, I saw a bursting bud, which held the promise of a joyful reddish-yellow flower. Calendula. My flower. Named, Aunt Charlotte told me last year, because it is the flower that blooms for the longest in the calendar year. Here it was, she was giving it to me.

"Now, Cal," Aunt Charlotte said, getting my attention

by tapping me on the head, "later on, I will show you how to make a healing paste out of the flowers, but for now, just learn how to grow them."

"Thank you, Aunt Charlotte," I said. "Where should I put them?"

"A nice sunny spot will do." Then she gave me a funny look and said, "Shall we go find a place together?"

"Yes ma'am, I would like that," I told her truthfully. I picked up the box of plants and with Aunt Charlotte leaning slightly on my arm, we walked around the path that leads along the dormitory side of the building. "There is my room," I pointed it out to her.

Aunt Charlotte stopped a moment and gazed to the window I had indicated. She turned around and looked about her. "It would be good if you could see the flowers from your window," she said. "Often, I mean."

I said nothing but looked about too. In the space before the gardens, near the first shed, Aunt Charlotte found a home for my calendula, just by the corner of the shed. That way, she said, they'll get plenty of sun, but still be protected from the worst of sun or rain. "Plus, you can see them." She had me run up to the second floor to make certain this was so before she produced a trowel from the depths of her dress, and directed me to dig a hole. "Now you make sure you water them good every day till they get good and settled in," she cautioned me.

"Yes, ma'am," I agreed. We planted them in their new home and I could see right away she had chosen well. They looked just right there, like they belonged.

"Cal, your mother named you after a powerful plant. It is also a cheerful and a hardy one. Calendula is a great healing herb and a beautiful, sturdy flower. She would want you to have some if she were here."

"Yes, ma'am, and if she were here, I wouldn't be here," I reminded her.

"Well," she growled, "I guess that's true enough, but don't be moping, baby. King sends his best. That dang fool is up hobbling about to every bit of trouble he can find. Don't forget the water."

"Aunt Charlotte, thank you, thank you," I cried, feeling sad that she was leaving. Tears welled up and stung my eyes. She had come to see me, to bring me a present. My own namesake flower, calendula. Then, as Aunt Charlotte and Abel drove off, I did cry for a few moments, sobbing until I could grab hold of myself.

I ran back to the shed and knelt in front of the calendula flowers she had brought me. The orange blossom was pushing forth into bloom on one of the tallest of the plants. It was a joyful, unruly color and I suddenly loved my name.

Chapter XVIII

A Trip to the Theater

Exams were held in April. I braced myself, hoping I was prepared to face this and bring honor to Mama and my pa. Somehow them being dead made me feel like it was all the more important I do well in school. This is hard to explain. Mama was kind of a scholar. Not only was she a Freethinker but her father and brother and grandfather were all college professors, and Pa, although not as educated as Mama, was mighty smart and valued learning. They wanted me to go as far as I could with my education. All my life they both told me how lucky I was to be of a new generation of Americans, who would be judged by their accomplishments rather than their ancestors.

Mama and Pa both believed that people had to be educated to take part in a democracy. Otherwise, only the rich who are educated will know what is going on in the country. They told me over and over that being an American was something to be proud of. Pa wanted the idea of democracy to be taken seriously. He stood up for the poor people, the slaves, and the outcasts. I don't know if I can be as outspoken as he was, but it is a part of my heritage. Mama was never as angry about anything as Pa but she spoke her mind whenever she felt like it. Pa used to say Mama was the smartest woman he knew. Back when they were happy, he was proud of her and her education. Later—well, later after one venture after another failed—everything made him mad and miserable.

I would like to be like Mama, smart and educated both, and have my opinions and speak my mind and sound intelligent. I miss Mama and my pa. Have I said this before? A hundred times? A thousand? A million times? In the meantime: back to work.

Matron had me out in the garden every day now for hours on end. We got ready to plant beans, tomatoes, and corn, and she had me weed out her flower beds. She sent Sylvie and me to New Market to do the shopping for the orphans. We bought forty pounds of potatoes and fifty pounds of wheat flour, five pounds of sugar, four pounds of salt. The boys from McCalla's, where we shopped, hauled everything over to the Asylum. I felt trusted by Matron to be put in charge. Being from a family that used to do business in New Market, I know where to go for a good bargain, and she knew that. From her expressions when we returned, she was pleased with our expedition.

One afternoon at the market, I saw Aunt Charlotte and King for a few minutes. They both seemed well, which cheered me some. King was back working for the city, digging graves and postholes and ditches once again. He was healing fast, no doubt because of Aunt Charlotte's curing ways—that, and wanting to get back to his own house so he could drink! Aunt Charlotte gave me a plate of poke sallet and it cleaned me out, as she no doubt intended. "Spring cleaning," she always says, "inside and out." Little did she realize I had to run down two flights of stairs at the orphanage to get to the water closet. The Ladies kept talking about getting one of the architects in town to put in water closets on all the floors. Dreamer! I could just wish.

It turned out I did very well on my exams and I was one of five orphans picked to go to the Lyceum to see a play by William Shakespeare. "Calendula Farmer," Miss Teaberry's voice read out in her dulcet tones. Lucas was picked too, plus Ann Waters, Tony Diamond, and Walker Taft. We all had to stand up at morning chapel when our names were called. Oh hurray! I wish Ma could know of this. It would make her happy to think of me going off to the theater.

I wore my blue stuff dress with a white apron. It was clean and ironed and ready. Mrs. Alice gave it to me as a goodbye gift. (She must have made it for me in her "spare time.") My only hat was my bonnet, and although I wanted something fancier, needs must, as Mama used to say. Josephine and Sylvie were jealous that I was going to the theater and who could blame them? They pestered me with questions and promises.

That day the five of us who were chosen were dressed

and ready to go by seven. Matron gave each one of us the up and down and passed us after we had corrected any spot of dirt or hairs out of place. We were a clean and carefully dressed quintet of orphans that climbed into that beautiful carriage. It had leather on the seats and something like velvet on the walls and thick warm curtains on the windows. This palace on wheels was driven by an old black man whose name I didn't know.

We climbed in and sat almost completely without talking the whole way into town. It's no great journey, only a matter of a quarter of an hour or so, but for chatter-bugs like us, the silence was significant. Lucas looked well with his hair combed down, although you could see, even in the carriage going over there, it was starting to become unruly. He had his cap on in the buggy. He sat across from me on the carriage seat and caught my eye so many times, I started blushing. Walker and Tony sat next to him. I sat with Ann. The night was chilly but we were all so hot with excitement I do not think we felt the cold.

As we pulled into the bright lights of the downtown, I could see many other carriages like ours. There were vendors on the street selling flowers and newspapers and hot potatoes. We passed Postlethwait's Tavern and it was lit up like daylight. There was music coming from its doors. In front of the Lyceum, we stopped, and were delivered to the front walk. Mr. and Mrs. Hunt-Adams, Mrs. Clay, and Mr. Henry Clay himself then collected us.

I had to remember to close my mouth at one point,

so stunned was I by all the attention. Not only that, but the magnificence of it all. If only I could describe to you the crystal chandelier, with its twinkling lights casting lively shadows. The room, and what a room, a hall really, so gracious and big, framed by carved faces and scenes in the corners and along the ceiling. We were being gazed at by satyrs and cherubs and angels and cows and birds and I can't even begin to tell it all. Let me say this: it was beautiful but a bit overwhelming.

At first, I was not aware of anything but the crush of people in fine suits and dresses and long warm cloaks. The smell of cigars and perfumes and champagne was so strong and surprising I began to feel light headed. The five of us found ourselves holding hands so as not to be lost in the crowd. We were taken to our seats. It was a profound relief to sit down in semi-darkness, to collect myself and recover from the jostling of the crowd. I am a child of the streets, jostling is nothing to me really, but the smells of this crowd, so sparkly and expensive, were not as familiar to me as the smells of sweat and old pee. This place had its own aromas, very strong and disconcerting, but also wonderful, beautiful, alluring.

I was seated between Ann and Lucas. Everyone was very careful to be on their best behavior. I was scared to death I might do something like break into a fit of hysterical laughter or crying. It's a terrible thing, but the more I try to control myself, the more likely I am to do something outrageous, egregious, outlandish, something seriously inappropriate. That is exactly what I struggled with that night, sitting in the lush and plush seats of that sparkling theater. Not to whisper, giggle, snort, shout, or in some other way draw attention to myself.

The lights went down, we in the audience weren't on anymore, oh blessed relief, no one could see us as we sat there watching these incredible players as they came on stage to transport us to another world. A world of fantasy and mythical happenings. I am not able to really appreciate William Shakespeare. Much of what the actors said went straight over my head. Still, I appreciated the song of their voices, the swank of their moves, the flush of their costumes and the sweep of the play. "As You Like It" it was called. Frankly, I don't know if I liked it or not, but I loved it.

During the intermission, the ladies and gentlemen stood and circulated in slow velvet and silken circles around the main room. This place was so seriously lovely that I did not know what to do except look and look and try to remember. But for what good? I cannot give you the real picture of the elegance, the perfume, the special sound of a crowd's intermission talk. The ladies fanned themselves, and the gentlemen stepped into the barroom for a drink or two. The five of us orphans stayed right where we were, not saying a word and trying not to catch each other's eyes.

It made me fair amazed that there are places right here in this town of the kind of loveliness we saw that night. The ladies' brocades stitched in gold thread, deep crimson and light blue, colors I don't even have words for. There were chandeliers swaying gracefully in the center of this huge arena, and paper on the walls with paintings and etchings of men and beasts and all manner of things. It is a wondrous place, and even if I don't understand Will Shakespeare all that much, I did so love being there and breathing the air and seeing the sights of the cultured people of this town. Their chatter is as loud as anyone's, but more refined like. It really does sound different than the crowd at the New Market at high noon.

When we were going home, Lucas sat next to me in the carriage and took my hand into his. This I could feel over and over, the calluses on his hand, the warm places and the sort of sweaty ones. He smiled at me with those sad eyes of his, and I fair swooned. I did hold myself together, however, and did nothing but enjoy being connected with him. It was at that moment I doubted my desire to teach and finally felt what might be called "the urge to marry."

That evening at the theater was truly an opportunity. I haven't told it all or well enough, but it turned out to be the kind of night that will live in me a long time, coloring experiences, heightening my awareness. It was a great kindness of the ladies to let the five of us go. I was already beholden to them for giving me schooling and board. I wish I could see my way straight into what I want to become with these chances, but I am completely unsure. I am too tired to think much more about it. What fun to imagine myself a teacher, a doctor, or an actress. But what is possible?

XIX

Asylum

I saw Lucas going out to the barn as I was coming in, carrying a churn of butter. He stopped and looked at me. I stopped too. We both started grinning like fools and couldn't seem to stop.

"Hey, Cal," he said at last.

"Hey Lucas," I said back, dimble-spoken as ever.

Then he blurted out, "Are you busy after church? On Sunday?"

Church, Sunday—I hardly ever went. Usually I went to the field or the forest to avoid it, with Matron's permission. (In this regard, I secretly suspected that Matron was a bit of a Freethinker herself.) But free after church? "Sure," I told him, "that would be fine."

"I'll see you then," Lucas said.

"Yes," I said. This is the way all of our conversations went. Stilted and jagged and incomplete. Still, I would rather we talk a little than not at all.

That Sunday I met Lucas after church, just like he said. I didn't know what to do, so I just lined up to go to church when Matron rang the bell. It was a long tedious service, but the organ was grand and the singing was rousing. I liked being able to stand up and sit back down. Afterwards, I walked out the long dark aisle and out into the street. There, off to a side, stood Lucas. He came and put his hand on my elbow, and in this way guided me down the block. We didn't say anything, just walked together.

When we had gone a little way, we stopped in front of Morrison College. Lucas said, "Look at that, Cal, it's called Gratz Park." He pointed to a green space that had been groomed and shaped, with a fountain and a gazebo. About a block down or so was the mansion estate of John Hunt-Morgan, who is doubtless some kind of kin to my Hunt-Adamses. It was a lovely park, and I said so.

Lucas took my hand. "Cal," he said, very soft like, "would you like to be my girl?"

I had wanted him to ask me this very question, but now, by some idiotic twist of fate, I said, sounding like an old prune of a woman, "What does that entail?" *What does that entail?* Had I lost my mind? I heard myself talking like a school marm at the very moment he was asking me to be his girl.

To give him credit, he considered my question and gave me what I took for an honest answer. "I don't know," he said. Then he grinned and I was truly lost in the good nature of that smile. There was something about that boy that just drew me to him. Then the whistle blew and we lined up to walk back to our home, our asylum.

There were two asylums in Lexington at the moment: the Orphan Asylum and the Lunatic Asylum. I studied the word "asylum" one day. It means a safe place, a refuge. I suppose ours was. A refuge I mean. All of us were orphans of one kind or another. By taking care of each other, we were taking care of ourselves. It is what Matron had stressed from the very beginning. Help each other. Work together.

The Lunatic Asylum was over off what they are calling Fifth Street, and it had been there for almost ten years maybe. It was a spooky place; there were overgrown evergreens down there and you could hear human wailing that sounded like wolves or witches or something scary. Some of the orphans had a bet to sneak out and go listen on the midnight of a full moon. I was one of them and I heard it myself. It gives me chills up and down just to remember it. I remembered a passage from one of our literature pieces about the shrieks and cries of Bedlam, Our Lady of Bethlehem, the asylum in London, England, that has such a reputation as to be mentioned in stories.

Lexington's Lunatic Asylum is the second in the nation; I heard Mayor Charlton Hunt proclaim it so in a speech he gave at the courthouse sometime back. He seemed to think we should be as proud of our Lunatic Asylum as the city is proud of how it is providing for its orphans with the Orphan Asylum. I have passed the Lunatic Asylum several times during the day, and even if there are screams or shrieks or other sounds coming from there, it doesn't bother me. But going there at night, on a full moon—it was a stupid gamble. What do those people need with a merely inquisitive spectator? I was ashamed of myself for going to spy on them. Not only did it scare me half to death, I felt bad for invading lives, for acting like their pain was for our amusement. The sounds were scary and torturous, and very, very human.

Miss Teaberry's school was ending in a few weeks. We would have what she called a summer term to help us be ready for the Common School in September. I had already learned to keep on with my reading and writing, and I certainly intended to do so. This is something Mama planted in me like a seed that grew roots. Get all the education you possibly can, keep learning, no matter what. We had a guest speaker one day after school which was rather thrilling. He was a poet from New York City. He came to Lexington to learn about horses. He read us poems he had written. My mind went into a drift and I enjoyed it immensely, if understood only a little. He had a lovely deep resonant voice, like the bottom of a bell.

My continued work in the garden left me sore and sunburned. I remembered a cure of Aunt Charlotte's and began soaking comfrey leaves and putting them on my neck and arms. It helped some with the sunburn. I had to ask the little ones not to hug me though, which they loved to do. They were rambunctious and forever jumping on me. I took them out on walks in the afternoons. That seemed to be a good combination because there was always something to look at and talk about, but at the same time they were using up some of their go. The only rough spots were when we got down on Cross and Main. There are a lot of carriages, wagons, carts, and riders. Getting my group across the street was not my favorite part of the trip.

We went by the farriers on Saunier Alley and I saw Brother Moses there. He was the black minister who buried Lawton, and I introduced him to my group of children. He let us come in and look around. They loved petting the horses and so did I. We also went to the New Market, but it gets so busy I was always afraid I was going to lose one of them. I suppose I could tie them together as I've seen some people do to their children but I couldn't do that, my Freethinking soul rebels at the thought of restraint.

The summer days fell into a pattern so completely different from June a year ago when Mrs. Alice and I huddled in the basement and listened to King's death cart clomp along collecting bodies. Now, I worked the garden in the early morning before classes, which were only for a few hours, and then afternoons I spent in excursions with my group of orphans. After dinner and chores, I had my time to myself, and most summer nights were passed like this one—writing. As I collected my thoughts and journal entries from the summer, I could see the past sliding into the present.

One Tuesday toward the end of June was maybe Josephine's birthday. (She isn't sure and there's no one to ask.) Sylvie and I gave her ribbons for her hair. She has such glossy black hair. Elf hair, we called it, but really I don't know why. She is such a quiet child. No one hardly ever notices her during the day, in the schoolroom or doing her chores. She is dutiful and hardworking, and ever so quiet. In that place of a hundred or so children, a quiet child was appreciated and quickly overlooked.

I think Sylvie and I knew Jo best of almost anyone there, because we saw the part of her she could not keep quiet and under control. Her nighttime self was a lively, angry, loud, and restless soul. Her daytime self was obedient, quiet and quick to fade into the background. That is Jo. That is one way she is like an elf—she fades into the trees, the bark, the sky, the grass, the scene. She draws no attention to herself. At night, she groans and protests the way her life is going.

I don't know what Josephine thinks, only that on this birthday she was (maybe) nine years old and a total orphan in this world the same as me. She could just as easily be ninety as nine. The child is old, old, old in her ways. Sylvie and I figured if we didn't celebrate her birthday, who would? But we were wrong. Matron gave her an unexpected piece of pie, which made Jo smile, but I knew she couldn't eat it. She has a light stomach and can only take so much at a time. She is a mighty small bit of a girl, but she made it to nine, and as I said then, "May her good fortune continue."

Josephine lost a tooth one day and I became the "tooth fairy" who left a penny under her pillow. Mama used to do this for me and had Jackie lived, I would

182

have done it for him. Instead, well, that night I sat at my desk, watching the sun set from my window, and most importantly waiting for Jo to go to sleep. She was snorting, and turning, definitely drifting off to sleep. I heard her mutter what I think was "Dammit, go away," but I am not certain. She doesn't talk like that when she is awake and neither Sylvie nor I would ever think of telling on her for what she cries out during her so-called rest.

The sun was going down to the west, but there was still light. It was quiet except for the chittering squirrels and the frantic mockingbirds out the window. They raised quite a racket, even this close to night. When Jo was definitely asleep, I went off to be the good fairy with my penny.

My class graduated from elementary school: Sylvie, Lucas, Tony Diamond, Ann Waters, and me. I asked Miss Teaberry to recommend me for the advanced track and she said she would. I explained to her about Mama's Freethinking and how she always told me my education was a lifelong responsibility. Miss Teaberry said my mother was ahead of her times, and it was a good plan but would be difficult for a woman.

I got to sing "My Country 'Tis of Thee" for an assembly. President Jackson never came near Lexington after the cholera hit. My voice had changed a bit as I continued to grow but I did my best:

183

My country, 'tis of thee,
Sweet land of liberty
Of thee I sing;
Land where my fathers died,
Land of the pilgrims' pride,
From every mountain side
Let freedom ring.
My native country, thee,
Land of the noble free,
Thy name I love;
I love thy rocks and rills,
Thy woods and templed hills;
My heart with rapture thrills,
Like that above.
Let music swell the breeze,
And ring from all the trees
Sweet freedom's song;
Let mortal tongues awake;
Let all that breathe partake;
Let rocks their silence break,
The sound prolong.
Our fathers' God to Thee,
Author of liberty,
To Thee we sing.
Long may our land be bright,
With freedom's holy light,
Protect us by Thy might,
Great God our King.

Such a celebration of freedom—I had grown to love the song and I was proud to sing it.

Looking back on what I have written, I have to say: Babble, babble, what a dreamer. Like my pa. I am Calendula Farmer, an orphan girl of poor parents, one of whom was known, toward the end of his life, as a drunk. What kind of life is out there for me? I don't know. I can do laundry and help in the kitchen; I can garden and sew, but not fancy work. I love reading and writing, collecting words and dreaming. I can't quite see the future of it all. Nor do I dare look too hard. If nothing else, I have learned that my life can turn its course, can change direction in a heartbeat, without warning. All of us at the Orphan Asylum had to let that in. I could hear the little ones crying at night down the hall. Truth is, there was a lot of crying at night, not all of it from the babies.

One evening as Sylvie was coming back from a visit with her family, a man pulled her into the bushes and assaulted her. I'm not even sure if she told Matron, but when she got back, she climbed into bed and just rocked herself for hours. She had been so scared and hurt. From then on she got what I call the panics. It would just come over her and she wouldn't be able to catch her breath. Her nights were particularly hard. Our cots were close, three of them lined up on the wall. I was the middle one and if I put my hand on hers and held it there, after a while she would calm down and could breathe again, although her breath would be shuddery and light for hours more.

Lots of nights I lay awake, not sleeping, just listening to Jo mutter, laugh, argue, and moan, but not cry. If she did cry, I didn't know where or when. It wasn't in our room. It was no wonder the child was so little, she worked all night tossing and turning, and ran off whatever biscuits and butter we could get in her.

When the calendar moved to the very end of June, I knew Rose was one year old. Somewhere up North, I hoped. I wondered what she had for breakfast. I wondered what little words she could say. I wished I could see her toddle around. Oh well. I didn't know if she would grow up knowing the story of her birth, how she was named after a flower, after her mama and me. How her mama was running, trying to get free when she died. No baby can remember that first long night of her life, but hers was spent in Appleman's Alley, under a full moon, with her dead mother's head on my lap, and it's one I will never forget.

Chapter XX

Changes

One day, I walked the children over to see an old friend of my pa's, the inventor Mr. Clayton. His workshop is truly wondrous. He has tanks of things he calls gas, and gadgets and baskets and balloons. He is always very jovial and cordial to us. (This was a two-for-one word. When I looked up "jovial," it said "cordial," so I had to look that up too. It all means warm, loving, kind, welcoming…from the heart. Which is Mr. Clayton to a tee.)

As soon as he saw us in the doorway, he bade us come in. We sat on a bench and he talked with each of the children. They conducted themselves pretty well. Frankie was swinging his boots and kicked Mr. Clayton in the shin. After his first wince, he mussed Frankie's hair and smiled at the boy. I've told Frankie not to swing his boots like that, now he can see why.

Truth to tell, one of the reasons I took the little ones out was to give them some exposure to people who might adopt them. It would be good to know they were in a home with loving people who actually wanted them for something more than their ability to milk a cow or pull a plow. Matron turned down some offers from people she didn't think would treat "her children" right. We had a staunch defender in Matron.

It had occurred to me that Mr. and Mrs. Clayton would be just a perfect home for some of my charges. How about Carla and Darla, our twins? They were both smart as can be and willing to learn. They were no trouble at all and could even be of help, given the chance. I just knew it. Our Jo could use a home, a real home—not that the Orphan Asylum isn't "real," it's as real as anything else, but Sylvie and I are not her ma and pa. Josephine doesn't have anyone. Neither do the Claytons, as far as children, I mean. So it seemed to me they'd be perfect for each other.

Jo, however, didn't make much of an effort to make herself look winsome or attractive that day. If anything, I'd say she was in a bit of a pout, but I don't know why. She said her feet hurt so I knew I'd better check on her boots, but even so, a little effort to act interested and grateful wouldn't hurt. All in all, however, the little ones did well. Mr. Clayton complimented me on them and bade us come again. He was hoping to have an exhibition soon, of some of his wondrous inventions. He said it might be in Gratz Park, perhaps as soon as next year. We thanked him again and set off home to our tea.

My calendula bloomed! Tomorrow, there will be more of the same in the garden. I am awestruck by how much some of these plants can grow, just overnight. The whole world is moving.

Lucas came to see me when I was in the cookhouse. He had grown or I had shrunk, and I think it was him. He looked happy and well. I guess he's growing into his ears.

"Cal, hey," he said.

"Lucas, how are you?" I was surprised to see him.

"I came to tell you, I'm not going to be at school next year. I got an offer for an apprenticeship. I'm going to work at the farriers, on Saunier Alley."

"At Strohmann's?" I asked and he nodded yes. "You're leaving?" I asked, feeling stunned.

He nodded yes again.

"So you won't be going to school with us next year?"

He shook his head no. For a while neither of us said anything. It wasn't an easy silence but I didn't know what words could fill it. Finally he said, "It's a good offer. I can make a living with the horses."

It was my turn to nod.

"And I like them," he continued. "Horses, I mean."

I nodded again. "I know someone who works there," I said, eventually. "Moses, Brother Moses Fisher. He's a minister, lives off Jefferson. For his day job, he shoes horses. He's a free man."

"How do you know him so well?" Lucas asked.

"It was when Lawton died," I said, shuddering back in my memory to that day. "That's when I met him."

Lucas shrugged and turned away. "I've got to go, Cal, but I wanted you to know where I am."

"Much obliged, Lucas," I said, feeling like an idiot. "Will you be rooming over there?"

"For now, yes. But... I will be back on Sunday, if you'd like to..." He was blushing and suddenly I was too, I became just consumed with a burning rash. "Maybe we could take a walk," he suggested.

I agreed immediately. "Yes, that sounds lovely, perfect." *Please stop talking, Calendula*, I yelled at myself, but no, I was suddenly the gracious lady who can't be quiet. "Marvelous."

Lucas looked at me oddly. Perhaps he had heard how truly false and ridiculous I sounded, but luckily his gaze was also fond. If the apprenticeship was to his liking and he signs the papers, he could have a trade in seven years. He would be twenty-two.

I wondered what would happen to me. Miss Teaberry did recommend some of my classes be at the college, but to what end no one would venture. I decided to accept my good fortune where I can find it, and hope that a purpose and a meaning will be revealed if and when I am able to appreciate it.

The chance to take art and literature classes at Transylvania and Morrison colleges was a true bit of luck. I wondered if I might sit in on any of the anatomy classes. I knew that as a girl, I would be banned by reason of my supposed delicacy. But actually, working with Aunt Charlotte has whetted my hunger for knowing about healing. She knows herbs, and she also knows bodies, and well, people. Transylvania College has a medical department that is known throughout the country. I have not only heard this from countless sources, I also read it in the *Gazette*. So, I would like to sit in on a class of anatomy. I would even like to study dissection. (Oh lord, why do I have such an unladylike and ghoulish nature?) At any rate, such choices are not available to me.

Several times during the summer, I assisted Dr. Rank in the children's clinic. We saw lots of children with summer colds, itchy eyes, draining ears, and crawling lice. Again, I was amazed at the number of broken bones that had never been fixed properly. These children lived hard and rough, and we were seeing the result. A number were limping on ill-set legs and probably would for the rest of their lives. There were several fingers flying at odd angles, and one child's collarbone had set at a wrong angle and she could barely look up because her back was so rounded.

I was given a job setting out bandages. I am not faint at the sight of blood, and crying may make me cry but I can still hold them down while the doctor looks at them. I have seen more death in my time than I ever wanted to, but in a way I feel at ease with illness. Too bad I couldn't be a doctor. Still, I liked helping in the clinic, and Matron herself told me I did a good job.

Independence Day—July 4th, 1834—was celebrated in Gratz Park. There was a parade with all of the notable people of the community. They had the senator Henry Clay, and the mayor Charlton Hunt, and guess who rode in the mayor's buggy? King! King looked right content with a cigar in his mouth. They were followed by the Hunt-Morgans and the Hunt-Adamses and the veterans of the Revolutionary War, and guess who else? The Orphans. We were cleaned up and brought out to march in the parade.

I did not appreciate being paraded like a spectacle. I kept thinking Mama would have been so embarrassed and Pa would have been so mad, but since both of them are dead and I am indeed an orphan, even though my face flamed a bright and painful red the whole way, I did my duty and paraded down Main Street, proof positive of the successful efforts of the Ladies. We were cleaned up quite thoroughly before being allowed out the door. I felt I had no choice and I have always hated that feeling.

After the parade, however, my day cheered up. Down at Postlethwait's, there was a champagne dinner for the finer people of the town. At least the richer people, that much is for certain. They arrived by horse and carriage, rugs were rolled out to receive them, and a man played a violin as they walked into the dining area. The park was filled with all kinds of amazements, including something they were calling electricity. It made sparks and seemed a bit frightening to me. Jo, however, loved it and wanted to learn how it worked. I preferred the display of farm machinery; there were newfangled plows and a chaff separator that operated with a foot pedal. There were steam-powered engines like the ones that will run the trains. Mr. Clayton was there with some of the machines from his workshop.

192

He had a balloon he says one day will carry people. In the air! Oh, there was a lot to see. Sylvie "fell in love" (according to her) with a quilt done by some ladies down in Frankfort. To me, it looked like a quilt. "To each her own," as Matron says. We had a long and happy day. I saw Lucas from a distance but I don't know if he saw me at all. He looked well.

That night I heard explosions of gunpowder from down at Lowry's Field House. They were shooting off these things called firecrackers. From my room in the Asylum, I could hear the explosion, and then sometimes see a flash of light or color in the sky towards the Field House. Then I could hear the dim roar of the audience. I do not much care for things that make loud noises and startle. I know some of the boys snuck out to see the show. Sylvie may have. Jo was sleeping quietly for once while the sky around us cried and screeched.

Chapter XXI

A Happy Surprise

Sometimes Josephine made me feel very old and wise and I was enjoying it tremendously. One day she saw me gathering the rags I use for catching my courses and she asked about them. I was embarrassed at first and didn't know what to say. I tried to hide them, but she'd already seen and wanted to know what they were. Suddenly I realized, she didn't have a mother anymore. I might be all she ever learned about it and I really didn't know much either. Just that it started happening to me last year, and stopped when I was weak and sick and has been going along about every month or so since then. I told her what little I knew.

"Is this going to happen to me?" she asked with a sense of dread in her voice.

"Yes, probably. Later on," I said. I learned this from Aunt Charlotte, that all women have this, that it has to do with having babies, although I didn't know what.

"Are you all right, Cal?" Jo asked, looking at me with concern.

"Yes, Jo, it's natural, there's no real harm in it, just a bit of a mess."

"Does it hurt? To lose blood I mean?" she looked at me hard, her eyes slantier than ever.

"A little, sometimes. Sometimes, no. It just depends."

"Does Sylvie?" she asked, looking over to her bed.

"That's her own business, just as it will be yours and nobody else's when it happens to you. Just as it would have been my own had a little girl not gotten nosy." I was gently teasing her, and she knew it.

"How do you clean them?" she persisted.

"Good grief, Jo. How do you think? In soap and water. I keep these rags separate and use them only for this. Enough with your pestering questions, now," I said, only half pretending to be angry.

"Don't be mad," she said in her soft little girl voice.

"Oh, come on, I'm not mad. It's just personal."

"Thank you for telling me about it. I mean it, Cal, I sort of knew a little bit, but I never saw the rags before. I wondered about that." She gave me an impish grin.

I burst out laughing. "Here's what else I know since you're so curious. They say your courses will sour the milk, but I know for myself that's not true. I've milked plenty of times when my courses were running and when they were not, and the only time the milk sours is if someone leaves it out in the sun too long."

Jo laughed and I went on with my chores. I admit it made me feel good to tell her something she wanted and needed to know. I liked being her big sister.

Two days later Mr. Clayton came by wanting to adopt an orphan—but the one he wanted was me. Me! I was open mouthed, stunned, and stupid when Matron told me. I actually got dizzy and sat down.

"What?" I asked.

"He wants to adopt you," she repeated. "His business is a bit chancy, him being an inventor, but this is a new age, there may be something to all these newfangled things." She glanced at me sitting across the table in the kitchen. I managed to shut my mouth.

"Me?"

"Yes, Cal. You." She looked at me closely. "What's so strange about that?"

I shook my head, as there was no way to explain it.

"Well, you think about it," she said, "and we'll talk some more later. I expect you'll want to talk to him. I gather he was a friend of your father?"

"Yes, ma'am." I really couldn't say more. I had to think and asked for permission to walk in the orchard.

"Yes, go. Might do you good," she replied, looking at me through puzzled eyes. Maybe she was as confused as I was.

Much as I had hoped for Mr. Clayton to adopt one of us, I wanted it to be one of the little ones. Oddly, I felt protective of my family, of Mama and Pa and Jackie. I hadn't realized it before but I really didn't want to be adopted. Maybe I'm too old. I don't know. "Write down your thoughts, daughter," I could hear Mama's voice. "You are entitled to the full of them and there's no better way to know them than to write them." I miss

Mama something awful. I don't even have a picture of her, no likeness at all, and that grieves me sorely. But I took her advice, heeded her voice and wrote out my thoughts, and in doing so I came up with an idea.

Maybe I could ask Mr. Clayton if he would take Jo and me together. And then I thought of Jo. What did she want? Funny, I hadn't really asked her. I guess we all assume that since we're orphans, we want a home, but I had surprised myself that day by realizing that isn't completely true, at least in my case. I know I'll never have my family back on Second Creek. Mama, Jackie, and Pa are gone, but I wasn't so certain I was in a hurry to replace them.

Then there was another voice in my head that said, "Ah, wouldn't it be lovely to have a home again. Not to sit at meals with a hundred other people. To have someone looking after me. To be somebody's daughter."

Then my mind rebelled because I already am somebody's daughter. I will always belong to Mama and Pa. This was a very confusing and distressing business. I was seeing so many sides to something I never expected to deal with at all. I will at least talk to Jo and see what she thinks, but no, wait. What if she wants it and Mr. and Mrs. Clayton don't? I shouldn't get her hopes up, if hopes they be, prematurely. For a while, I must do nothing but let the news sink in. Being a Freethinker can be absolutely exhausting at times.

That night, I listened to Jo tossing and turning, mumbling and moaning her way through the night.

The next day, I walked to Mr. and Mrs. Clayton's house on Mill Street. It sits next to his workshop and is a modest but neat brick house. I patted my hair down and straightened my dress before rapping on the door using the brass knocker. It was opened by a maid, a woman smaller than Matron by many pounds, but about the same age and white.

Not having a card, I simply said, "Calendula Farmer to see Mr. and Mrs. Clayton, please."

She looked me over from tip to toe. "What is the nature of your business, Miss Farmer?"

For a moment I just stared at her, but then I collected my wits and said, "It is personal."

That seemed to be satisfactory for she left me in a small vestibule and presently escorted me into a room quite unlike any I had ever seen. There were tables and chairs and bookshelves and footstools and a piano and potted plants and great glass cases with what must have been Mr. Clayton's inventions. I couldn't even tell what else was there, but it was a great jumble of things. At the Hunt-Adams's everything had its own room. This was like several specialty rooms crammed into one that was not really all that large.

I was shown to a settee and asked to wait. Soon, Mr. and Mrs. Clayton came in. They rushed over to me and I came to my feet. "Oh, Calendula," Mr. Clayton said, grasping my hands, "does this mean yes?"

"No," I said, rather louder than I meant to. Both he and Mrs. Clayton looked a bit taken aback. "I mean, not for sure," I said, in a softer tone.

"Of course, of course," Mr. Clayton said. "We must talk. Mrs. McKeever told you of our wish to make you one of our family?"

To this I could only nod. For a moment I completely forgot that Matron's other name was McKeever. I took a breath. I had to muster my courage and speak.

"Sir," I began, "and Madam." I nodded at Mrs. Clayton who had not said a word the whole time but who never took her eyes off me; it was as if I were the most interesting thing she'd ever seen. I took a deep breath. "I am not prepared to accept your most generous and thoughtful offer without more time to consider it." This much I had rehearsed in my mind on the way over, but for the rest I didn't know what I would say.

"We want you to continue with your schooling at least for the next two years," Mr. Clayton said. "I know your parents wanted you to get all the education you could."

I was glad to hear this, having wondered if they just needed me for maid help. "The thing is," I began, "there's another girl there, a little girl, Josephine, she's nine, we think." I swallowed and kept going, "The thing is I've been thinking…" That was as far as I could get. It wasn't really a stopping place, but there was nothing more I could manage to say.

"Ah," said Mrs. Clayton. It was her first word, if a word it is.

"Well, see, I haven't talked to her about it or anything, I don't even know if she'd want to come here, I mean even if you would see fit to have her." I knew I was rambling, babbling even. I stopped, hoping one of them might take the lead. But no, they simply looked at me expectantly. "The thing is," I said, repeating myself, "I don't know if I might not be too old to be, well . . . adopted. Nothing personal, but Jo might, well of course I don't know, but she might fit in better, being younger and all, if you see what I mean?"

Mrs. Clayton nodded at me encouragingly but said nothing. Mr. Clayton merely stared. Silence can be compelling. I seemed unable to resist filling it.

"It's not that I'm not grateful," I continued, "and honestly, if you all need me to help out here," I glanced tactfully around the chaotic room, "I'd be more than happy." I paused. I was exhausted so I quit trying to fill up the quiet. I had simply run out of gumption. I couldn't say another word and signaled this by shaking my head.

For a long while the three of us sat in silence. Finally, Mr. Clayton turned to his wife and said, "Shall we have tea, my dear?"

Mrs. Clayton nodded and rang for the maid who appeared quickly enough that I, being wise to the ways of servants, wondered if she hadn't been listening just outside the door. "Tea, please," Mrs. Clayton told her and the maid nodded and withdrew.

Again, the three of us were alone, sitting close together but not speaking. At last, Mr. Clayton said, "Well, Mary, I shouldn't mind another girl but, of course, it's up to you."

Mrs. Clayton nodded her head but maintained her impressive silence.

I broke in. "If you want Jo, I'd come and train her, I mean if you think she needs it. She's a good girl, very smart and quick to learn. If anything, maybe a bit moody. She's the only one left of her people. And, of course, if you don't want me, I mean after this, well I understand." *Quit talking*, I was yelling at myself in my mind, but I didn't seem able to stop.

"Nonsense, my dear," Mrs. Clayton said quickly in her lovely rich voice. "Of course we want you too. I mean, we wanted you all along and we still do. But it doesn't have to be as a daughter. We would simply like to look after you. That's all. Edward knew your father, and I knew your mother. I thought very highly of her."

Compared to what had gone before, this sounded a very long speech for Mrs. Clayton, and I tried to respond in some way.

"Mama was a Freethinker," was what came out of my mouth.

"Indeed she was, and a rare thing that is on this earth," said Mrs. Clayton.

I smiled at her. It felt so good to hear someone say something good, just plain good and kind about Mama. She was right too. Mama was a rare thing on this earth. "Mrs. Clayton," I began, and then stopped. I could not think of what to say. Finally I managed to say that much. "I don't know what to say."

She did not need words. She is not that kind of woman. In fact, she is spare with them herself. Eventually, she said, "Calendula, bring your Jo here tomorrow, if you can. It seems this might work out."

And, indeed, it did seem so. Jo thought the idea of the two of us living with the Claytons was excellent. "Yes!" she cried. "They could be my mother and father and you could be my sister," she reasoned.

The Claytons were not wealthy people like the Hunt-Adamses, nor were they poor. They were middling. The house was attached to his inventions shop, which really is a wonder to behold. It is not a large house, but there is room enough for both of us. Jo and I would have beds in a room with a window that looks out onto Mill Street, the veritable middle of town. I could watch as the buggies go by, the horses prancing, people walking on the street. Nonetheless, I will still need to go to the orchard for peace and quiet. I had learned that about myself.

Mrs. Clayton does most of her own cooking and sewing. Jo and I will help with the work, but also go to school. For this I am thankful. Jo is a smart little girl and needs to keep learning. I may not become a doctor, but Miss Teaberry gave me a Latin dictionary to help me learn the origins of words. I love how tangled up they are with each other, and how almost every word has its own history. Just like the rest of us.

Besides the maid, whose name is Mrs. Shelby, there is Mr. Shelby, her husband, who works in the shop and does most of the heavy work around the house. The Claytons are white people but they don't have slaves. I'm glad for that. After seeing Lawton die, I did not want to be a part of this "peculiar institution."

The subject of slavery, and especially how to stop it, was much on my mind. I could not and cannot to this day get it out of my mind as the wrong thing that it is. It's not only because of Aunt Charlotte being like my second mother and Rose and Rosalie and what happened to Lawton, although that's a big part of it. It's just the more I think about it the more I think it's cruel: one person owning another. My parents were against it, and my grandparents as well, all four of them from what I've been told. They were from the North, Boston and Philadelphia, and up there, people don't agree with slavery the way they do down here. I was raised in our family to think of it as an aberration of society, something we would hopefully get over soon, like a bad flu or an infected sore. In time, with care, it would be healed. But I saw no sign of slavery declining in Kentucky any time soon.

In fact, the more I studied on this, the more I was convinced that if a white person is rich enough to own a slave, in Kentucky, he will. Even if he thinks slavery is a "peculiar institution," as Mr. Henry Clay calls it, he still has slaves. I was reading an essay on liberty by Thomas Jefferson, but the whole time I kept thinking about how he owned slaves. What about their liberty? This is the part of me that thinks and reads and studies. The other part of me has these flashing images of Lawton coughing his life away after being beaten and dragged to death. Of seeing him laid out in that dark little cabin and Mr. Hunt-Adams saying, "It'll cost me a packet." I remember that little slave girl with "HC" branded onto her skin. These pictures come and go like strikes of lightning. I admit I was confused as to what it all meant but basically I just knew that slavery was wrong. Just as I know it today.

Some people say slaves can't take care of themselves, that they need a keeper. But how can that be true when someone like Aunt Charlotte, who was a freed slave, had made a life respected by everyone, no matter what her color? People of this city, black and white, tipped their hats and nodded their heads out of respect for her. And why not? Between her baking and her doctoring, not to mention her Christian faith and her kind nature, Aunt Charlotte helped the lives of hundreds and hundreds of people in this town. Once when I was going on about my feelings, Sylvie told me I sounded like an abolitionist, which upon reflection, it turned out, is exactly what I am.

Chapter XXII

The History of My Life So Far

Again, an earthquake in my life, a sea change is how Matron put it. Moving this time to a new "family." Not a servant, not an orphan, a member of a family. Even if they aren't mine, they kind of are now. Mrs. Clayton is quiet and somewhat shy, but as I've gotten to know her over the last few weeks, she's opened up with me. She speaks rarely but has a lively look of attention in her eyes so I feel like she's all there. Mr. Clayton is a spirited man and the life of the household. He is cheerful and optimistic. I can't wait to see if his balloon can fly.

Still, although I am happy, or happy enough, I am lonesome too. Not just for Mama and Pa and Jackie, but for something else that I can't name. I've spent this last week assembling my scribbles and writing out this history of my life so far. I feel better having it all in one place at last.

Lucas seems to have taken up with one of the Strohmann girls. I think her name is Berta. I heard talk of it, and it hurts, truth to tell. I went to church to meet him a few times but he didn't come. Then I heard the rumor about this auburn-headed Berta, and I finally put two and two together. They're living right in the same house there on Saunier Alley. He might have had the goodness to come and tell me himself, but he didn't.

Another page in the story of my life so far is turning. I will begin anew, this time with a sister of sorts, Josephine. Mr. and Mrs. Clayton will be my guardians, not my mama and pa. They want to help me, and whether I care to admit it or not, I can use all the help I can get. Even though they are gone now, Mama and Pa left me plenty to grow up to and think about.

On our last night at the Orphan Asylum, Sylvie came home early from a family visit to spend time with us before we left. She was actually happy to be getting the room to herself and who could blame her, but it was a little sad for all of us. She told me she thought she might get married when she turned sixteen. She has a male admirer named John Carpenter. I'm not sure how they met, but she is always singing his virtues. I hope she does have somebody to hold hands with in the dark when her panics come. I told her about how Lucas never saw me anymore, and she told me she pretty much had guessed it. She said she was sorry, and suddenly I said, "I can live with it." And I meant it.

Aunt Charlotte and King came by together on that last afternoon, and I met them in the kitchens. "Girl child, you still scrawny," said Aunt Charlotte. "What am I going to do with you?" King nodded hello and I returned the gesture. He looked older somehow. Maybe having that broken leg and having to put up with her cures for two months had aged him.

"Aunt Charlotte, do you know the Claytons?" I asked.

"Some," she said. "Enough not to worry about you going there, if that's what you're getting at."

"I mean do you know where they live?" I clarified.

"Of course I do. Everybody knows where he has that inventions place on Mill Street. Why, you better believe I know where you going, girl." She eyed me head to toe, then took my hand in hers. "Cal, we'll come by. You my baby, now, girl. Don't you forget it. I loved your ma and honey, I love you."

She had never spoken so openly to me and I began, without warning, to sob. King stepped up and began patting me on the back, as if my sobbing were the hiccups. It helped some but I continued to weep, quietly as possible into my apron. I felt bereft. I cried for awhile and King patted me and Aunt Charlotte stood there holding my hand. In time I quieted and Aunt Charlotte brewed me a tea for my nerves. I think it was chamomile and tasted kind of bitter.

I told Aunt Charlotte I want to be an abolitionist, and she told me the first thing I needed to do was learn how to keep my mouth shut. "Less said the better," she told me. For me, that's a hard one, but I do come by it honestly, after all, look at my parents. They were both known for speaking their minds. And truth to tell, I am an abolitionist and I intend to do something about it. It is not only a peculiar institution as Henry Clay and other rich white people would have me believe, it is an evil one. Of this, somehow, I grow daily more and more certain. I remember how Aunt Charlotte spirited Rose away, *poof*, the baby was gone North to safety. There are ways of getting people out of slavery and I intend to study on what they are. I am a white girl who has a lot to learn, but I know right from wrong on this one. That's one thing my Freethinking has brought me to.

I had been saying goodbye to my little ones and my friends at the asylum, saying my prayers as best I could, remembering my family. Matron came in to say goodnight. I missed her already, though she will just be a bit across town, Sylvie too. And Cook will be at the Hunt-Adams house on the hill, and Mrs. Alice. Most important for me, Aunt Charlotte and King were still on Town Branch, living in uneasy harmony, but both loving me, and me them.

Jo held out her hand to me before she fell asleep. She said, "Cal, I'm scared. What's it going to be like over there?"

I thought about that a long time, feeling her skinny cool fingers in my hand. "I don't know for certain, Jo, but I'm hoping for the best."

"But Cal . . ." She paused. I waited. "I'm scared."

"Me too, but we'll be all right. I can almost guarantee it." I sounded rather hearty and false to myself.

"Almost," she echoed quietly, "but not for sure."

"No," I admitted.

We were quiet for a while, just swinging our hands in the air between our cots.

Then I told her, "Jo, whether good or bad comes to us, you and I are sisters now. We're just going to hold hands and go on." I gave her hand a squeeze. "What else can we do?"

"Exactly," she murmured and relaxed into sleep.